EARL OF GRIFFITH

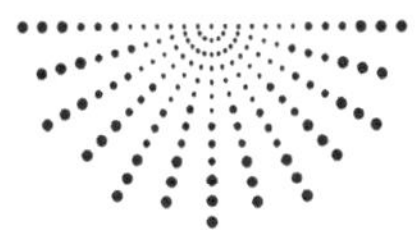

AUBREY WYNNE

PLATO PUBLISHING

ISBN: 978-1-946560-26-1

Editing by The Editing Hall
Cover Art by Jaycee DeLorenzo

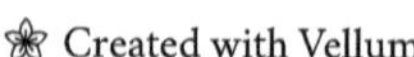

HISTORICAL ROMANCE SERIES

Keep updated on future releases, exclusive excerpts, and prizes by following my newsletter:

https://www.subscribepage.com/k3f1z5

Once Upon a Widow series (sweet Regency)

Earl of Sunderland #1

A Wicked Earl's Widow #2

Rhapsody and Rebellion #3

Earl of Darby #4

Earl of Brecken #5

Earl of Griffith #6

Beware A Wallflower's Wrath #7

Read on Kindle Unlimited

A MacNaughton Castle Romance (steamy Regency Highland series)

A Merry MacNaughton Mishap (Prequel)

Deception and Desire #1

Allusive Love #2

A Bonny Pretender #3

SUMMARY

The Earl of Griffith

Sorrow and Regrets...

Lady Helen was a young, naïve girl when she gave up everything for a charismatic Irishman and eloped. Finding herself a widow after a few short years, she is disillusioned with love and raising a three-year-old daughter alone. Her homecoming will be bittersweet as she faces her family, asking forgiveness for the lies and the worry she has caused. But her first encounter in England isn't with a family member. Helen's brother has sent a handsome Welshman to fetch her, and he soon charms both her and her daughter.

An unexpected ray of sunshine...

Conway, Earl of Griffith assumed his title and Welsh estate at birth. His world is gray, full of responsibility, and lonely. Griffith agrees to help a friend by escorting his sister from Bristol to London. At first sight, Lady Helen illuminates his dull world, and her daughter adds laughter to his life. But he senses the woman's haunted eyes are not only from grief and wonders what secrets she holds close to her heart. As his affection turns to love, Griff must find a way to convince the beautiful widow that love is worth another chance.

A sweet Regency romance.

PROLOGUE

April 1816
The Irish Sea

Helen lifted her head to the biting winds of the Irish Sea. Rory's warmth soaked into her back as the sails popped and snapped, the ship tossing on the angry waves. She smiled as her new husband's arms held her tight, watching the port of Holyhead and Wales fade from sight.

"So, I spent my last coin on the cabin. We'll be alone tonight. No steerage class for Mrs. O'Neill," he whispered into her ear.

Mrs. O'Neill. She was thrilled each time she heard the name. Turning around, Helen wrapped her arms around his neck, letting her hood fall to her shoulders. "I love you, Roarik O'Neill."

"But am I worth losing yer family for?" He nuzzled her neck, and she closed her eyes with a sigh.

"You are exactly what I wanted," she reminded him, snuggling closer. "My father's ire will cool, eventually. Mama will make sure of it."

Her words sounded more confident than she felt. The Earl of Stanfeld would be livid when he found out his youngest daughter had eloped at sixteen with an Irish bastard of a duke. Helen had pleaded with her father.

"He's half English, Papa. His father is a peer of the realm." She clutched his sleeve, her eyes sparkling with tears.

"You are much too young. Your mother wants you to have a Season next year. I don't understand the urgency of a union unless—"

"Papa, how could you think such a thing?"

"How could you think I would allow you to marry the man? He's baseborn and not even acknowledged, you little nodcock. The man wants whatever money you can provide for his 'cause' and will stoop to any level to finance it." Lord Stanfeld paced the library. "He's involved with the Radicals in Dublin. A toady of O'Connell who only wants to make a name for himself."

"But—"

"He doesn't have a farthing of his own, Helen! Do you want to raise your children in some Irish hovel?" Her father jabbed a finger at her. "Over my dead body."

It didn't matter. She was in love with a man who cared more for her than a title or duty to the family name. Rory was nothing like her father, a man who viewed the world in black and white and saw only the practical side of life. Her husband was passionate, with no obligations to an old family name. Helen wanted to be someone's priority, not a broodmare to produce an heir.

She had saved her pin money for a year and stashed away the small amounts for "something special." Though she'd only known Rory a few months when he'd proposed, Helen had accepted immediately, thankful for the pile of guineas hidden in her wardrobe. After selling some of her jewelry and other items she'd never need, there had been enough to get started in a nice townhouse, with dailies perhaps for cooking and cleaning.Rory had warned her that it would be hard at first. She wouldn't have the luxuries she was used to. But they loved each other. It was enough, wasn't it?

The ship dipped and rose, a sprawling gray and white wave splashing against the hull. "I think that private room sounds like a good idea." Helen shivered as she thought of the wedding night to come. The thought of lying with a man for the first time, *this* man, both terrified and thrilled her.

He took her hand and placed it in the crook of his elbow. "My lady, yer chamber of marital bliss awaits." His hazel eyes sparkled, the familiar smile still causing her stomach to tumble.

"O'Neill! Here, O'Neill!" yelled someone on the crowded dock. A pair of men in dull brown wool jackets and pants waved in their direction.

"There they are, love. Joseph and Colin, my friends I told ye about." Rory waved back at his cronies, a grin transforming his face from handsome to boyish. "They're excited to meet ye."

They made their way through the crowd, down the ship's plank. Helen carried two bags, and Rory hoisted the trunk on his shoulder. She admired his upper arms straining against the thin coat as he dodged other men with barrels over their backs or lugging more trunks. Helen finally gave up trying to walk by Rory's side and stepped behind him, gripping the back of his coat as they picked their way across the docks. Introductions were made, and she was immediately relieved of her bags.

"Ye didn't tell us she was a beauty," said the dark-haired Joseph.

"Are ye sure she's English?" asked Colin, nodding at Helen's ruby-red hair.

"I'm half English. My mother is a Scot," she told them with a laugh.

"Now I like ye even better," said Colin, his own red hair barely tamed beneath a wool cap. Then he turned to Rory. "There have been some happenin's while ye were gone. I hope ye had a grand time because it's time to get back to work."

Helen followed the three men away from the ships and took her first good look at her new home. With a start, she realized there would be no carriage to pick them up. The streets were crowded like London, though the buildings were not as tall. After walking for close to an hour, they turned down a narrow street. The rows of houses all looked the same, with a layer of grime covering the steps and brick. They climbed several flights of creaking stairs, and she fought the urge to cover her nose from the sour smell that seemed to permeate the halls. Her feet were tired, and she was ready for a hot bath, a meal, and a clean bed. And time with her husband to get to know her new surroundings.

Reaching a door chipped with paint and marked with a black **6**, Rory pulled out a key. To her surprise, Colin and Joseph followed them inside. They seemed very comfortable in the apartment, knowing where to put the bags, then making themselves at home at the table in the small kitchen.

"Now, I'm sorry, love. But I've got some business to take care of tonight." He tapped her nose with his knuckle and grinned at her. "Then we'll continue where we left off this morning."

Her cheeks burned with the memory of their intimacy. She was truly a woman. "I'll unpack, then. How shall I arrange for a bath?"

Her husband's chortle took her by surprise. "Ye're a missus, now. We left the grand Lady Helen behind in London, remember?"

"Are you saying a *missus* does not bathe?" she quipped, looking down at her muslin gown stained with street muck. "You won't love me for long if I begin to smell like the alleys we passed on the way here."

"Not to worry. I'll haul water for ye twice a month. Ye'll stay sweet enough," he said with a quick kiss on her mouth. "Make yerself at home, and I'll be done shortly."

It was close to dawn when Rory joined her in bed. Helen had lain awake for hours, listening to the deep rumbles of the men, occasional shouts, and bursts of laughter. *They haven't seen each other in two months,* she told herself.

But the *kitchen conversations,* as she began to call them, happened every evening. Helen found herself acting as a serving maid and feeding all three men most nights. Occasionally, others would join them. Fortunately, most meals—meat and bread—were bought already prepared and baked, and she eventually learned to appreciate the versatile potato. She didn't particularly enjoy the work, but it kept her occupied and was better than the alternative. If Rory and his comrades weren't in her kitchen, then they were gone until dawn somewhere else. She hated being alone more than she hated cooking.

Helen wondered exactly what her husband's *business* was. Rory was always evasive when she asked for more details. He had told her he was employed by a Mr. O'Connell as a driver and messenger. That he kept odd hours. He had also taken her purse of coins and "deposited" it for safekeeping.

After six months, Helen realized she was never going to live in a townhome with a daily to help her. She was the only servant who would be cooking and cleaning. The money she'd so carefully saved was gone. She suspected it had gone to "The Cause" that dominated Rory's life.

"Now, love, to be sure, we're doin' so well here," he would croon in his soft, low brogue. "We won't be needin' any strangers in and out every day. And I'm so proud of how well ye're copin' with yer new surroundings." Then he would kiss her, take her to the bedroom, and make her forget all her carefully worded arguments.

Helen laid her hand on her stomach, cradling the restless babe inside her. Her father would have been pleased to know she was so fertile, she thought ironically. Disappointment threatened her composure, but she blinked back the tears. Rory and the others would be home soon, and she needed to get the potatoes on to boil.

She shuffled from the tiny bedroom, no longer hearing the creaking beneath her, through the modest sitting room with a rag rug and two wooden rockers, and into the small side area called the kitchen because it had a stove for heat. Scooping coal from the bucket, she poked the fire to life again. Then she sank into a sturdy but nicked-up chair and sobbed.

Rory's first priority was not her, but his beloved Ireland. He cared for her, but now she understood that marriage to an earl's daughter allowed him a certain respectability with the local magistrates. Because of his titled English wife, they would assume he accepted the British monarchy and its stipulations. But if her husband had to choose, the rights of his fellow Irishmen would come first. After all her careful plans and promises to herself, she'd married a man just like her father.

CHAPTER ONE

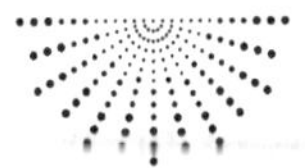

Late June 1820
Dublin, Ireland

Helen sat up in bed. The furious pounding began again. Her hand slid across the cold sheet next to her. Rory hadn't come home. Maeve began to cry, and she scooped up the three-year-old in her arms. The loud tattoo continued as she tried to get one arm into her robe, switched Maeve to her other side, and finished pushing her other fist through the scratchy wool sleeve.

"I'm coming," she called in a shaky voice, patting her daughter's back in an attempt to calm her. Her chest tightened with each step. Something was wrong. She felt it in her bones.

Pulling open the door, she found Joseph's wife with her fist in the air, ready to knock once again. Her brown eyes were wide with worry, her hat tilting precariously on her mop of umber waves. "Helen, ye must get packed. There has been a terrible… accident, and ye must be away or—"

"Where's Rory?" Her heart pounded at her friend's hesitation. *"Where's my husband?"* she screamed, now in a full panic. Maeve began to cry again.

"Shush, now. He's dead. Ye must listen to me!" Maire grabbed Helen's shoulders and shook her lightly. "There was an argument in the pub. A pack of Loyalists heckling the Nationalists. Rory tried to break up a fight, then took it outside. When The Force arrived to restore order, yer husband accidentally shot one of the Peelers. Another Peeler shot Rory in the back when he tried to flee the scene."

The Peace Preservation Force—begun by Sir Robert Peel, the previous Chief Secretary for Ireland—consisted of officers and a magistrate who acted as a traveling militia to deal with and trouble. The Peelers, as they became known, were dispatched to squash any rioting or unrest. Murdering a Peeler was a serious offense and could be interpreted as treason. Especially by a well-known Nationalist, such as her husband.

Dead? She bounced Maeve, soothing the child's cries and following Maire to the bedroom. Her only friend reached under the bed, pulled out a traveling bag and a small trunk, and set it on the rumpled sheets.

"Give me Maeve and pack what ye'll be needin' for a few weeks, including yer tickets for England. I'll explain in the hack." Maire reached for the whimpering girl. "I'll gather some food for my little darlin'."

Twenty minutes later, Helen sat in a filthy, rented hack, trying not to take a deep breath. The stale smell of vomit permeated the air, and her eyes stung from unshed tears. She had to be strong for her daughter.

"Explain to me why I must leave. I'm now a"—her voice caught as she struggled to maintain her composure in front of Maeve—"widow with a child and no money. I'm not even involved with his doings."

"Rory was known as one of the leaders of the Nationalists in Dublin. The authorities don't know he's dead yet. Joseph managed to get him away from the fray, but it was too late. He died within an hour of escape." Maire squeezed Helen's hand. "My Joey says they'll come after ye. They'll want to make an example of Rory, dead or alive."

"What could they possibly do to me?" Her head was spinning. A dead husband, a crying babe, and midnight conspiracies. What had her life become?

"Put ye in goal for interrogation. Ye have no family here to protect ye. Maeve will be taken from ye." Again, Maire squeezed her hand. "I know ye were plannin' to go home for yer brother's wedding. We'll exchange the tickets ye bought for a ship in Cork. There may be eyes at the Dublin port."

Everything was happening so quickly. If it weren't for the jarring hackney ride, Helen would think it was all a bad dream. Somewhere in the back of her mind, she'd known it would come to this someday. Her passionate husband would have never settled for growing old peacefully.

What had been her last words to him? Had they been loving or dismissing? Both seemed to come out of her mouth in equal amounts lately. Tears burned the back of her eyes once more. She leaned her head against the cracked leather of the cab and swallowed back her fear. Maeve was her main concern. Her precious, blue-eyed girl with the midnight curls of her father. Helen's own father had died a year after her elopement. Another man Maeve would never know.

She hugged the plump body now softly snoring against her chest. At least Helen had a father during her childhood. Who would step into that role for Maeve? Her brother, Gideon? The burning in her eyes began again. *NO!* There was no time for grief now. Later. She'd think about this tomorrow.

"What is our destination now?" she asked Maire.

With a relieved sigh, her friend began, "First, we'll stop at a coach inn just outside of town. I've a bit of coin for anything ye need before boarding. I assume yer brother will care for ye once ye reach the English shore."

"I must send a letter to Lord Stanfeld," she said, wondering what Gideon would think when she came without Rory. She smoothed her skirt with a shaky hand. "He thinks our family is arriving at Holyhead and going straight to Scotland for the wedding. I need to relay my new port of arrival and request an escort of some kind."

Maire nodded. "Aye, now ye're thinkin'. That's my girl. Ye can post yer letter from the inn." She pulled a sugar cube from her pocket and handed it to Maeve to suck on. The girl made a happy mewling sound and began gnawing on the sweet. "I'll stay with ye until Cork and make sure ye board with no troubles."

Two hours later, Helen's hand trembled as she signed the letter.

Mrs. Roarik O'Neill

The contents and signature made it seem as if Rory were still alive, and she was still a young, happy wife and mother, not a grieving widow. She closed her eyes, remembering his smile and the glittering green eyes that always shone with excitement.

But her husband had also been a radical, a man convinced Ireland should be independent. Adamant that the Irish were equal to any Englishman, thus deserving of the same rights. His passion and self-righteousness had been his undoing. It had taken her more than a year to realize she had been in love with the charming persona of Rory. That he had used her as a guise for respectability. Why would he be conspiring against the Loyalists when he had an English wife? The daughter of an earl, no less.

Of course, he'd been *fond* of her, and the physical attraction had blinded her for a while. She'd been so naïve in the ways of love. But his devotion to Maeve was undeniable. He was—had been—a good father when he was there. Rory had loved his daughter with the same passion he had loved Ireland. Almost.

"Would ye like me to post that for ye?" asked Maire. She sat in a chair next to the small hearth in their room. "It may take us several days to reach Cork. I assume ye want the letter to reach the family before ye make shore."

"Yes, thank you," Helen agreed with a smile. "You've been so very kind and patient, Maire. I will miss you."

This kind woman across from her had been Helen's saving grace for the past few years. Maire had swooped in like an angel, showing her where to shop for produce, who had the best prices for meat and bread, and becoming a loyal friend. She'd also helped deliver a bawling Maeve. After having two sisters, Helen was used to company and conversation. Though Maire worked as a seamstress by day, she always stayed with Helen on those nights when the men were "out."

"What will happen to Rory's…" *Body.* She couldn't say it out loud yet. It didn't seem real.

"My Joey took him to our local parish. The priest will bless him and make sure he's buried proper." Maire pulled her chair beside Helen and laid an arm around her shoulder. "And I'll be sure to tend that grave like I do my da's."

"I don't think I'll ever return," she whispered, leaning her head against Maire. "Am I deserting him by not coming back to Dublin?"

Maire shook her head. "Ye've done enough for him, my dear. He wouldn't be expectin' ye to do any more than ye already have. There's Maeve to think of now. She's the most important thing."

"I'll make sure she knows who her father was. A man she could be proud of, who was loyal to his homeland until the end." Helen closed her eyes. No crying yet. If she opened that gate, she might never close it. Too many regrets, too many broken dreams.

"Sure now, let me have the letter and ye try to get some sleep. Ye'll be back with yer loved ones soon enough." Maire left, closing the door softly behind her.

It would be bittersweet to see her family again. Helen had thought she would miss the lively social events of London. Instead, she had missed her parents and siblings. The easy life of a prospective debutante, with no other worry except what to wear to the musicale on Thursday. She kissed the top of Maeve's dark curly head, her small chest rising and falling with steady breaths. Her daughter would love the upcoming adventure.

Helen had let her family believe all was well in Ireland. Her letters had always been positive, never allowing them to think for a moment that her life was anything but blissful. Even now, she omitted the fact her husband was dead. She had used work to excuse Rory's absence; he was needed by his employer. Her brother deserved a happy, carefree wedding. She wouldn't mar the event with her news. There would be plenty of time to tell her tale when they all met back at the estate.

Home. Oh, how she'd missed Stanfeld Manor. It was the first time in four years she let herself fully remember the place, let random images run through her mind. The gardens, the ice pond where she'd skated every winter, the stables with her favorite pony. Comforting memories that would see her through this next stage of her journey. Helen prayed the weather held. Once in Cork, the voyage to Bristol could take a couple of days or a week, depending on clear skies and the wind. At least she wasn't prone to seasickness and hoped her daughter would be the same.

When Maire returned, Helen had one more question.

"Did Joseph tell you if Rory said anything before he died? Did he think of me and Maeve?" she asked.

Her friend avoided eye contact and hesitated.

"Tell me, please." Perhaps there would be something to cling to in the dark days ahead.

"He was a patriot to the end, Joey said. His last words were, 'Keep up the fight.' And Joey promised him that they would."

Helen clenched her jaw against the onslaught of pain and guilt. Why would she expect anything else?

CHAPTER TWO

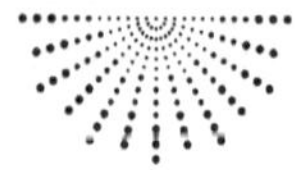

Late June 1820
London, England

"Welcome, Lord Griffith, welcome!" Gideon, Earl of Stanfeld rose from his chair behind the massive oak desk and came forward to shake Conway's hand. "Good to see you again. I trust you've been well?"

Conway nodded. "Aye, in more ways than one." He'd joined the drovers for this trip, bringing three hundred head of Welsh cattle to the Smithfield market in London. "My brother said you'd be in Town, so I sent a note. Thought I could buy you a drink somewhere along St. James Street if you have time before I go."

"Of course, but what's the occasion?"

"Since your estate manager shared some of his breeding secrets, the value of my livestock has improved the last couple years. Wales always had good cattle, but I'm a firm believer in constant improvement. Unfortunately, my fellow

Welshmen don't seem to be interested." Conway shook his head. "This last herd brought in a substantial amount. More than any of the neighboring estates got per head. I'm hoping this might change their mind."

"I'll admit I wasn't enthusiastic about animal husbandry, but my man Birks is a genius at it. Our sheep production has doubled since I gave him free rein." Stanfeld's raven hair gleamed in the sunlight pouring in from the window. He poured brandy into two crystal tumblers and handed one to Conway.

"To success and love," Stanfeld said with a huge grin, holding up his glass.

Conway laughed. "I'll toast to success but leave the romantic notions to you. I hear you're leaving soon for your wedding?"

"Yes, Lissie wanted to be with family and have a traditional Highland ceremony. She and Mama have already left for Scotland. I had an unexpected summons to Town and sent them ahead. I'll leave tomorrow, stop by my estate in Norfolk, then on to MacNaughton Castle to meet my bride." Stanfeld's mother was Scottish, and her ancestral home was where the earl had met his betrothed. "Both my sisters and their families here in England have already left. My youngest sister in Ireland will be landing in Holyhead next week with her husband and making their way to the Highlands."

"You'll exchange the heat and havoc of Town for scotch whiskey and worse weather, eh?" Conway enjoyed his trips, but nothing was better than the fresh air and rural views of his beloved Wales.

"Och, I spend more time on my braw estate in Norfolk than this *manky* city. I'll no' mind a wee chill over the numpties strolling through Hyde Park," said Stanfeld in his best terrible Scottish brogue.

"God's teeth, but that was horrid." Conway shook his

head and chuckled as he threw back the last of his liquor and accepted more.

The men chatted about business and mutual friends, finished off their brandy, and made plans to meet at Boodle's later that night.

❦

The gentlemen's club was busy, but there were still a few empty tables when Conway arrived. Though he'd truly enjoyed the role of drover and the satisfaction of bringing his own cattle across the border, it was time he dressed and acted as a gentleman again. He tugged at the form-fitting, deep-blue waistcoat and pulled at the cuffs still stuffed in his sleeves, thinking of the baggy pants and jacket of light wool that had left him so unencumbered. He had been restless as of late and decided an adventure would do him good. Had it?

His grandmother had been horrified he might sleep on the ground and mingle with *worse-than-commoners* for weeks. She had been somewhat mollified when he told her his coach and driver would be sent ahead to meet him in London. Yet, Conway had thoroughly enjoyed himself. He'd learned from his stepfather to appreciate manual labor, the fulfillment a hard day's work could provide a man. It also ensured that as a landlord, he would better understand his tenants.

Conway took in an appreciative whiff, his mouth watering from the well-prepared meal after weeks on the trail with basic supplies, bad coffee, and bellowing bovine. He tapped his rough fingers on the table, finished with the superb pea soup, and resisted the urge to smack his lips. But his stomach still growled as he waited for the roasted fowl, glazed carrots, and pudding.

"That looks better than a drover's fare," he said when a

plate was set before him. With his glass refilled, Conway inhaled his meal. Wiping his mouth with a cloth, he tossed it on his plate and gave a loud, satisfied sigh.

"That sounded like an excellent reference for the chef," Stanfeld said, approaching from the door. "You look to be a contented man, Griffith."

"Indeed, I am," agreed Conway. "And I have a decanter of excellent brandy to share."

"Don't mind if I do."

They sat in friendly silence while the waiter brought another glass and poured one for Stanfeld. The sound of men at the gaming tables cheering—or jeering, it was hard to tell—broke their quiet.

"How goes it in Wales?" asked Stanfeld. "I hope the countess is well?"

"My grandmother will outlive me," he said with a chuckle. "She's too stubborn to die until she's good and ready." Conway's grandmother still lived in the manor house with him. While there was a dowager house on the property, she had remained at the manor in charge of the household duties. Would she move willingly when there was a new countess? It was past time for him to marry. A fact that she now routinely reminded him.

"And your brother, Brecken? I haven't heard any news of an heir yet." Stanfeld smiled. Conway reckoned he was thinking of producing his own heir soon. "Though it hasn't been a year, has it?"

"No babe yet. They were married last September, so I wouldn't be surprised to hear some good news in the near future." Madoc, the Earl of Brecken was his half brother and lived a few days' ride or so from Gruffyd Estate. Doc's English bride, Evie, was lovely and vivacious. She was one of the few women Conway felt comfortable with.

"Any prospects for yourself, old man?" Stanfeld smiled

and held up his glass. "There's something to be said for the shackles when it's the right woman. You must be thirty by now."

"So I've been told," he said with a snort. "I've yet to find that woman. Agreed, thirty-two is a bit long in the tooth, according to many females, but I may still have a few more years of bachelorhood left."

"Don't like the idea of the parson's trap, eh, Griffith?" There was no judgment in Stanfeld's voice, only curiosity. "I used to have the same aversion."

"No, I truly don't have a dislike for the institution. I'm just not… comfortable with the ridiculous pleasantries we have to endure to find a bride. If I have something to say, I say it. If someone asks me a question, I answer it." Conway shrugged. "But to speak of this week's weather for a polite ten minutes, when it doesn't even pertain to the crops, seems like a waste of time to me. I either come off surly or like a green boy."

"I don't believe I've seen you in either light. When the right woman comes along, the words will flow." Stanfeld laughed. "Or you'll stutter like a dunderhead. Hmm, that could be a good wager for the Betting Book at White's."

"I'd prefer to *do* the wagering rather than *be* the object of the wager."

"I'll second that." Stanfeld tapped his chest, then paused, his smile fading. He pulled a letter out from his waistcoat.

"Bad news?"

"Not exactly. I received a letter from Helen, my youngest sister."

"The one in Ireland?"

Stanfeld nodded. "It seems she's coming without her husband. Rather than landing up north, she'll be arriving in Bristol for some reason. I need to find someone to meet her and accompany her to Stanfeld. My estate manager will escort her to the border. One of the MacNaughtons, my mother's family, will bring her from there."

"I'm heading home at the end of the week. I could go to Bristol."

Stanfeld's face lit up with relief. "Really? She should have a lady's maid with her and my three-year-old niece. I'd feel much better knowing a man was accompanying them."

"I'd be happy to. Give me the information and a likeness, and don't worry about her again." He had nothing waiting for him at Gruffyd Estate except his grandmother. The older he got, the more that seemed to bother him.

"It's settled then. I'll send 'round the information and a cameo with a small portrait. She doesn't take after me, though, except for the MacNaughton-blue eyes. Fiery red hair and petite, but don't let her size fool you. She's a spitfire." He shook his head, his blue eyes flashing. "The trouble she used to get into as a child… I was always keeping some escapade from my father."

"I'll keep a tight rein on her, to be sure."

"And you won't have to worry about chitchat with Helen. She'll blather on about any subject."

"Good to know." Conway smiled. This might be a nice diversion. The women would stay in the coach, so he wasn't worried about prolonged bouts of polite conversation. And he loved children. He could spend hours with the villagers' offspring, following him around, asking a hundred questions, and making him laugh at their honest and unique perspectives on life. Perhaps the child would enjoy a ride in the saddle with him.

The next day, Lord Stanfeld was true to his word. A letter with the approximate landing time, names, and a locket arrived at his hotel. He was in the dining room, still used to his country hours, enjoying an early meal. Conway clicked the button, and the small heart-shaped bauble opened.

His breath caught. Before him was the loveliest woman he'd ever seen. Ruby-red hair, sapphire eyes, and a smile that could seduce any man. Her complexion was creamy ivory, her throat slender and graceful, sloping to a full bosom.

Conway blinked and cleared his throat. *It's a painting, you Cretin!* Yet some invisible pull would not allow him to look away from Lady Helen's image. It was as if he'd always known her. Or was meant to know her.

He shook his head. He'd listened to too many Welsh superstitions and fairy tales. He needed a drink. Or a good night's sleep. Or both. What fanciful imaginings over a friend's sister. Who happened to be married with a child. *I'd wager the little one is as beautiful as her mother.*

That night, he dreamt of a ship on a stormy sea.

Lightning cracked overhead. Thunder rumbled over the cries of a woman. Conway tried to reach her on the slippery deck, calling to her as she gripped the rail. The rain slashed his vision in heavy sheets, and the next flash of lightning revealed the woman clinging to the edge of the deck. Her pale dress clung to her curves, and tendrils of red hair were plastered against her face and neck. He reached out to pull her to safety, but she shook her head.

A wave washed over the side of the ship, and he blew out a breath. She was still there, now crawling as the vessel tipped up, then down.

"Helen!" he called, blinking against the pelting rain. "Give me your hand."

When she looked up, the distress in her blue eyes squeezed his heart. Not fear. No, this woman was not afraid of going overboard. Such pain, such disappointment was etched into her face that Conway paused for a moment. She had the look of someone who'd given up.

He dropped to his knees and made his way to her side. "Come with me."

She shook her head again, backing away from him.

"We must get off this deck," he shouted over the snapping sails. He put an arm around her crouched body and pulled her close.

"I don't have the strength to face it," she choked out. "Leave me."

"Never."

Conway bolted up in bed, his breath coming in rasps, sweat drenching his nightshirt. What the deuce had he dreamt about? A woman he hadn't even met yet. *God's teeth,* he hoped it wasn't some sort of premonition like the villagers talked about. Some terrible omen that the ship he was to meet would sink.

He got up and put on his silk banyan, his bare feet slapping the rug as he walked to the side table. Pouring a glass of brandy, he sat down in front of the hearth and glared at the dying embers of the fire. Well, Conway knew one thing for certain. Mrs. Helen O'Neill had made a considerable impression on him.

CHAPTER THREE

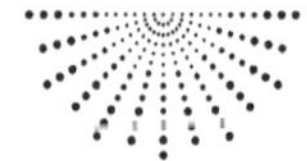

Early July 1820
Bristol, England

"Mama, I'm thewsty," said Maeve as she tugged on her mother's stray curl. They stood on the deck now that they were close to shore. Helen had stayed in the cabin, preferring to avoid any questions—or problems—about a woman and child traveling alone. The girl had loved the rough sea, giggling and squealing each time the ship had rocked. It had taken all Helen's patience to get her daughter to sleep last night. And her bright blue eyes had popped open with the dawning sun. Helen had only dozed, unable to close her eyes for long without images of Rory haunting her. His fist raised against another screaming man, or shot in the midst of the crowd, his cries of pain echoing in a murky alley as his friends carried him away.

"Yes, love. We'll get something soon. See the land?" she

asked, pointing to the gray horizon. "That's England, your new home. It's where your mama's family lives."

"Mama's family," she repeated in earnest. "Gwandmama Maeve and Uncle Gidjun."

"Yes, that's right." Helen wondered if it would be Gideon meeting her at the docks. Certainly not her mother, not when she had a long journey to the Highlands this month.

A gust of wind whipped Maeve's black curls across her face, and she laughed with delight as her pudgy hands pushed the hair from her eyes. "Big wind, Mama."

"A very big wind for a very big girl. Now we must go to our cabin and make ourselves presentable." She set Maeve on her feet and took her tiny hand. "Do you remember the way?"

They collected the traveling bag and small trunk, Helen's reticule, and Maeve's rag doll. Looking at the dingy, torn toy, she said, "Our first purchase once we're home is a new doll for you. Would you like that, my sweet?"

The toddler nodded. "But I keep Ahwohwah."

Aurora had been the name given to the doll when Rory had bought it for her birthday and Christmas, last December. Maeve had wanted to name the toy after her papa, but Rory had said it needed a girl's name. So, Aurora was decided on as a feminine form of Roarik.

Making their way to the gangplank, Helen scanned the busy dock. No one looked familiar. She watched a handsome man with raven hair study a pocket watch or locket, then peer at those waiting on deck. After the third time, she realized he must be meeting someone he didn't know.

At that moment, their eyes met. His midnight gaze widened, then he slowly raised an arm and waved. *At her.* Her stomach did a ridiculous twist as he made his way up the gangplank. He was of medium height with a stocky build. Helen thought of the boxers at Jackson's. And handsome in a rugged way, not preening like the London dandies. His umber suit was well-made, tailored, and of expensive material that stretched across a broad chest.

A friend of Gideon's, no doubt.

"Mrs. O'Neill?" His soft, deep timbre dripped over her like warm honey. He held out his hand. "The Earl of Griffith at your service. I've been honored with the task of escorting you to Stanfeld Estate."

She breathed a sigh of relief and immediately trusted the man. He spoke with a Welsh accent, so Helen assumed he was acquainted with Gideon through business. Taking his offered hand, Helen introduced herself and her daughter.

Lord Griffith squatted closer to Maeve's height and held out his hand once again. "It's a pleasure to meet you, Miss Maeve."

"You have eyes like a cwoh. Shiny," replied the little girl, leaning closer to study the man's eyes. "I like shiny."

"Maeve, it is not polite to compare a man to a crow." Helen turned to Lord Griffith. "She loves birds, so really it was meant as a compliment."

He seemed a bit taken aback but recovered quickly. "Well since you approve, I suppose I'll keep them. I'd considered trading them in for a pair of blue like yours."

"Do you think mine aw shiny?" she asked, reaching out a finger as if she'd poke his eye, then traced one of his thick black brows instead.

"I think your eyes sparkle like the finest blue gems," he answered with a smile.

Maeve giggled at that. "Mama, he's nice. Will we live with him?"

Lord Griffith coughed and choked, holding back a laugh. "I think your uncle would prefer you stayed with him. Though, you would definitely be welcome."

He stood, retrieved the meager luggage from her side, and

held out his elbow. Helen took Maeve's hand, and they made their way from the ship. "Shall we wait for your lady's maid and the rest of your luggage? Or is it being sent ahead?"

Helen blinked. How much should she tell this stranger? Nothing about her recent widowhood. If she spoke of it, she'd overflow the Thames. Not only from grief over a dead husband, but from the sorrow of years lost and starting over. The heartache of her daughter growing up without a father. "No, er, yes, It's all been sent ahead. It's just the two of us, and I have what I need for the ride home, thank you."

Her one evening gown and three day dresses had been sold long ago. The simple sturdy skirts she wore now were typical of any middle-class working woman. Clean, at least, she reminded herself, saving her Sunday best for their arrival. But her own wardrobe was in storage. Her mother had told her in one letter that she would keep Helen's dresses in anticipation of her daughter's return. She had brought more clothes for Maeve than herself but knew the child would need some made at the rate she was growing.

"Our coach is just over there." The earl pointed to a black vehicle with a coat of arms on the door. It had a white shield with two red dragons. Above the shield was a knight's full helmet; red and white leaves grew out of this, leading to yellow daffodils. A driver sat on the box, four matching bays in hand.

Walking between sailors and hired men hauling shipments, avoiding the mud when she could, Helen felt her head spin. She'd eaten or slept little in the past two days, and the cacophony of the docks, the smells of sweat and animal dung, all seemed to invade her head and stomach. Her body was giving out, even if her mind insisted it didn't need rest.

A small dog barked from atop a wagon, its stubby tail wagging. Maeve wrenched her hand from Helen's. "Puppy!" she cried as she ran toward the animal. A hack passed in front of them just as Maeve dashed away. Helen screamed, the horse reared, and Lord Griffith dove in front of the cab. Covering Maeve's body with his, he rolled them both out of the path of danger.

Her entire body trembled, watching the pair rise from the dirt and mud. Maeve clung to Lord Griffith's neck, her tiny head tucked against his shoulder. Back at Helen's side, the earl's face held only concern.

"She's fine, no harm done," he said, attempting to give the child back to her. But Maeve clung tightly to him, and Helen shook her head.

"I d-don't think I c-can hold her," she whispered. The ground beneath her feet seemed to be moving. People were spinning past her at odd angles. Then blackness.

❧

Conway bent his knees and slid his free arm around Lady Helen's waist. *Lady Helen... Mrs. O'Neill, you lobcock.* He pulled her tightly against his side and looked at Maeve.

"I think Mama is vewy sleepy." She reached out and patted her mother's head. "Can you cahwy Mama too?"

"I'm afraid not, little one. One rider at a time." He nodded to the driver, who hurried over. "Would you hold Mr. Thomas's hand so I can help your mother to the carriage? Then she can take a nice nap while we drive."

"I could sit on you shouldahs," she bargained. "I'd be vewy still."

"I'm sure you would be, but I think we'll try that another time. Thomas?" Conway tilted his head toward the girl. "Could you take her, please? I believe we're in need of smelling salts."

"Got a flask of cheap whiskey if it'll help." Thomas took Maeve, who immediately began petting the man's white hair.

"So soft," she said before sticking her nose close to his hat and scrunching her face. "But it smells like a hawse."

"And ye're quite the prize yerself, miss," Thomas answered with a chuckle. He began dusting the toddler's jacket before picking up the travel bag. "Ye're not smelling so rosy, either."

"Nor I, I'm afraid. At least it's only mud and no other muck." Conway was glad his valet had stayed behind. The condition of his coat would have sent the man into an apoplexy. Turning to the damsel in distress still at his side, he put his other arm under her legs and scooped her up.

She was petite, limp, and utterly divine. Her body tucked against his as if they were two missing pieces of a puzzle. Long dark lashes arced against her pale skin. Light freckles sprinkled her nose, and her lips were pink as the primroses in spring and slightly parted.

Good God, I want to kiss her.

He thought of his dream. How he'd tried to save her, and she didn't want to be rescued. Well, she'd had no choice today, had she? The thought made him smile for some reason.

After Thomas deposited the girl in the carriage, Conway ducked under the door and laid Lady Helen on the bench. Maeve sat down on the floor, next to her mother, and held her hand. He checked her pulse and noted her color was returning. *Good! Probably too much excitement.* He knew from his own mother that females could be fragile creatures.

"Why don't you sit up here with me, Miss Maeve? The ride could get bumpy."

Maeve shook her head, the midnight curls flying against her cheeks. "When I sick, Mama sits with me." She blinked, her blue eyes moist.

"And you shall be sitting with her. If you come up here, you'll be safe but still next to her. Your mama will want to see that you're well as soon as she opens her eyes." He held out a hand. "You don't want her to worry, do you?"

Maeve shook her head again and sniffed. "N-no." She dropped her mother's hand and climbed up on the bench next to Conway. "I want a nap too. Sing to me?"

The girl picked up his arm, wiggled underneath, and snuggled against his side with a yawn. To Conway's surprise, it felt right to have a child rubbing her cheek against his waistcoat. He began to hum an old Welsh tune that many considered their informal anthem. Her eyelids fluttered and closed.

While the other occupants slept, he was able to study both of them at his leisure. Their dress was not of the quality he would expect from a woman of her status. Perhaps because of the voyage and tiresome land journey, she'd chosen to wear more practical clothes. Especially traveling with a young precocious girl, who was apt to get dirty. He saw similarities in their pert noses, small chins, ivory complexions, and splattering of freckles. They had the same piercing blue eyes as Stanfeld. But Lady Helen's face was more heart-shaped compared to her daughter's. And Maeve would obviously grow taller than her mother. He would have guessed the girl to be closer to four with those long, spindly limbs.

His gaze returned to the woman on the opposite bench. A fierce protectiveness rose in him. He pulled the girl closer and watched Lady Helen's chest rise and fall in a steady rhythm.

He must have dozed, for his eyes snapped open at the sound of her groan.

CHAPTER FOUR

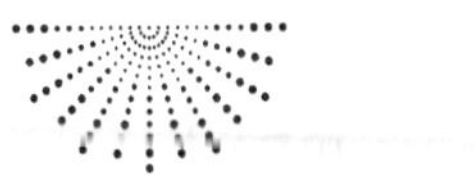

On the road from Bristol to London

Helen swayed with the rocking of the ship. It felt so good to just lie here, eyes closed, no worries…

Horse hoofs! There were no horses on a ship. She opened her eyes to see a handsome man smiling at her, and Maeve sleeping against his chest. *Gah! Where am I?*

The panic must have shown on her face because the gentleman spoke reassuringly. "Your daughter ran in front of a hackney, I saved her, and you fainted. All is fine, and we're on our way to Stanfeld Estate."

His voice was low and calm; it soothed her nerves. She sat up, smoothing back her hair, then tried to remove the wrinkles from her olive skirt and spencer. An impossible task. "Thank you," she mumbled and frowned. "I'm afraid I've quite forgotten your name. I do apologize."

"No need for that." He smiled again. A kind, genuine

smile. "After a long journey and such a scare, I'd be surprised if you did remember. I am the Earl of Griffith, friend and business associate of your brother. I must also apologize for this unusual situation, but I'd been told you would have a female companion with you."

"Fortunately, I'm not a debutante worried about my reputation." She managed to smile back at him before closing her lids against the pounding in her head.

"Are you sure you're fine?"

"Just a megrim." She opened her eyes again. "I want to thank you for saving Maeve. I don't know what I'd do if something happened to her. She's all I have—" Helen bit down on the inside of her lips.

She would keep her troubles to herself until after Gideon's wedding. No matter how sharp the pain in her heart. Her mother had always said sharing one's misfortunes lessened the suffering. Oh, how she wanted to lay her head in Mama's lap, let her mother share the burden of this terrible ache. The awful guilt. The painful knowledge that she only had herself to blame for her present situation.

Such an impetuous, stupid girl she'd been.

Then her gaze fell on Maeve. If she hadn't been impulsive and rebellious, she wouldn't have had this precious, loving child. With a deep breath, Helen scolded herself for the moment of self-pity. She was no longer a young girl. She was a mother with responsibilities. And her daughter was worth every tear, for Maeve gave back joy a hundred-fold with her smiles and hugs.

"I stopped on my way to Bristol and arranged for rooms at decent inns. I thought with a child, we wouldn't want to take any chances with unscrupulous patrons. We'll also have a private dining room." Lord Griffith paused and looked down at the mussed dark curls of his charge. "She's lovely. You must be very proud."

Tears threatened again, and Helen only nodded. What a considerate man. She was surprised that she liked him so quickly. Although, he'd already played knight errant twice. Almost as if he was born to the role.

She cushioned her head against the velvet squab, then turned, and rubbed her cheek against the softness. With her eyes closed, she reveled in the expensive fabric brushing her skin. It had been so long since… Helen jerked her head forward again, feeling his eyes on her.

"Will Mr. O'Neill join you later?"

She shook her head. His voice had the timbre of a baritone. Without reason, she knew he would sing beautifully. Then exhaustion claimed her again, and she soon lost the battle with her lids as they shuttered and closed.

"Mrs. O'Neill."

The baritone interrupted a lovely dream. She and Maeve were skating on the pond at Stanfeld.

"Mama, wake up. Wake up for the advenchah."

Helen peeled one eye open to see blue eyes and a tiny nose almost touching her own. Little palms squished Helen's cheeks. "It's called 'The Fox and Wabbit' and they have vewy good food and feathah mattwesses that will swallow me up."

"Mattresses that will eat you?" Helen asked, her "s's" having a pronounced slur with Maeve's hands still pushing on her cheeks.

"You silly, Mama. Lawd Gwuff said the mattwesses ah so thick that if I jump on one, it could swallow me. I will hide, and when you come in, I will jump up and yell, *SUPWISE*!" She giggled, then turned, and settled on her mother's lap. "I miss you, Mama, when you sleep."

"And I always miss you, my sweet," Helen whispered in her ear.

"That tickles," she said and laughed, rubbing her ear.

"And who is Lord Gwuff?" Helen asked, looking up at Lord Griffith as Maeve pointed to him.

"Guilty. It's an old nickname from my childhood. The Welsh name for Griffith is Gruffyd. As a boy, I tended to be serious, and my mother would sometimes call me Lord Gruff." He shrugged, his coffee gaze sending warmth through her. "My brother heard her once, and it became his favorite moniker for me."

"Did you grow into a gruff man or leave the solemnity behind with your boyhood?" She saw kindness and intelligence in his dark eyes, but there was something else too. Sadness? No, not exactly.

"I prefer to think I learned there was an appropriate time for being somber and for enjoying oneself." He leaned forward, his elbows on his knees, and poked Maeve in the belly. "You, young lady, are nothing but pure delight. I hope you stay that way."

"I like him, Mama. He's stwong and makes me laugh."

"Laughter is good for one's health," agreed Lord Griffith. "It frees the soul and lightens our burdens. Don't you think?"

His gaze locked with hers, and she smiled. "I hadn't thought about it. It's been so long—" Helen clamped her lips tight.

"We'll have to turn it into a science experiment. I'll find opportunities to make you laugh during our trip, and you can tell me if it makes you feel… lighter." When he grinned, a crease formed along one cheek. Too big for a dimple, but appealing, nonetheless. "Bargain?"

"Bargain."

Lord Griffith reached for his hat and plopped it on his head as the carriage rolled to a stop. "Will you do me the honor of dining with me this evening, Miss Maeve?"

"Sewtainly," she said, cheeks scrunching up with her big smile. "But you have to take Mama too. We ah two peas in a pod, and nothing will sepewate us but the good Lawd above."

"I shall bow to your wish since I'm not nearly as powerful as Him." With that, he exited the coach. Popping his head back in the open window and tipping his hat, he said, "I'll confirm my arrangements and come back to escort you to your room, ladies."

Helen said a silent prayer for sending *this* man. He seemed to enjoy his role of protector, and her resolve was fading. Leaving the details to him allowed her to save what strength she had left. And it would take every ounce of energy to hold herself together until she reached Stanfeld Manor and the privacy of her own bedchamber. Then she would let the tears fall and cleanse her soul.

He seemed destined to watch her sleep. They sat in front of the small fire, mother and daughter dozing. He studied Lady Helen's profile. Beautiful, proud, and... haunted. That was what he saw in the depths of those cerulean eyes. What had happened to her since she left the protection of her family?

It wasn't any of his business, of course. Yet, he was drawn to her and had the strongest desire to protect her and her precocious child. Granted, she was married. But it didn't matter. Keeping her safe and seeing her happy once again were his only concerns. He knew from her occasional smile and Stanfeld's description of her that Lady Helen had been happy. Her brother had described her as mischievous, intelligent, always questioning or arguing some point she'd read.

The sleeping woman next to him didn't seem to possess any of those qualities right now. Where were they hiding? *What* was she hiding? Conway had always been skilled at knowing when people spoke the truth. While he hadn't thought she'd outright lied, he was certain she hadn't been completely honest with her brother. Well, if she wanted to talk about it, fine. He wouldn't push her.

Maeve rubbed her eyes and stretched, pushing a fist against her mother's nose and waking her up with a start. Lady Helen looked around, eyes wide as if trying to remember where she was.

"Sleepy, Mama," the little girl mumbled.

Conway rose and picked up the toddler. "I'll carry her for you. I'm ready to turn in myself."

She gave him an appreciative smile and rose unsteadily. He caught her elbow and experienced the same rush of heat as when he'd carried her to the coach.

"You must be exhausted," he murmured over Maeve's head.

Lady Helen nodded as he followed her to their room. She pulled back the bedclothes, and he gently laid the sleeping child on the sheets. Conway brushed her damp curls from her cheek and tucked the counterpane around her small shoulders. When he straightened and turned, Lady Helen blinked rapidly and ducked her head.

He cleared his throat. "We'll leave first thing in the morning. I'm sure you're anxious to see your home." And then he'd leave her. That caused a sharp pain in his chest. *Ridiculous!* He'd only known her a day. Yet, from the moment he'd seen her image in that locket, he'd felt… connected to her somehow. An invisible thread that pulled them gently together.

You're the one who needs sleep—or a drink!

"Yes, I've missed my family, the estate grounds. It will be wonderful to see them again through Maeve's eyes." She smoothed her hair back and peered up at him, cheeks tinged pink.

"I'll leave you to your rest, then."

Just as he reached the door, he heard a soft, "Thank you." He nodded without turning around, quietly closed the door, and wondered how those two little words could fill him with such satisfaction.

Conway thought about his return to Wales. It had become a lonely place with just him and his grandmother. And Lady Griffith was not a warm person. Though she doted on her grandson, she had a reputation for being cold and unforgiving. His own mother had felt the sting of her disapproval most of her life.

His father had died before he was born. The widowed countess had found love when Conway was a toddler, but the dowager had refused to let Conway go with his mother. Her new husband, the Earl of Brecken had intervened. An arrangement had been made to accommodate both women. Conway spent half of the year—the warmer months—with his mother and stepfather. Brecken taught him how to be a good earl, to care about his tenants, the basics of farming and animal husbandry, and to never rush into a decision. In business or love. The colder months, when there was little to do on his own estate, Conway went home.

There, he spent long hours with Powys, his estate manager. They rode out so the tenants recognized their lord by sight. Powys had taught him that people were people, regardless of their heritage. "Everyone bleeds, my lord. We're all the same under our skin," he'd say when one of the villagers would make a comment that surprised their young lord. The elder Welshman also taught him that every decision Conway made impacted others that depended upon the estate. Whether it was the villagers or tenant farmers, Conway's resolutions of any given situation, directly or indirectly, affected them all.

He had learned much from his mentors. His stepfather was gone now, and Powys was white-haired and moving slowly. The steward was training his nephew, Owen, as his replacement. Conway liked the hard-working young man. They had tried experimenting with the cattle, and Owen's open-mindedness had been rewarded with larger, sturdier stock. And with that came bigger profits.

Gruffyd Estate was thriving, so why did he feel so hollow inside? Because he longed for a family, the sound of children laughing and playing in the halls of the manor. He wanted what he'd had only part of every year when he lived with his mother, stepfather, and half brother. He wanted the kind of marriage his mother had found with Brecken. But then the thought of a Season emerged, being on display, the ladies themselves parading before eligible men, hoping to find a match in their first Season. It was a horrendous ritual that he desperately wanted to avoid. There was also the inconvenience—for the potential female—of his being Welsh. It wasn't a popular destination for most women used to the excitement of London.

Perhaps he'd find a young woman he felt comfortable with, like Lady Helen. Though, he was certain it was the fact she was married that allowed him to speak with such ease. And the presence of the adorable Maeve. But this chance encounter had made him realize the empty feeling he couldn't identify was loneliness.

CHAPTER FIVE

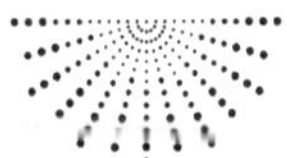

Helen blew a stray curl from her eye and furiously flicked her fan. It was hot. Unbearably hot. There was no light breeze as they'd had the day before. Today, either the windows stayed closed to avoid the dust, or the windows were down so they could breathe in the dust in exchange for a wisp of air. Not much of a choice. She gave her daughter an envious glance. Maeve rode in front of *Lawd Gwuff* on his big, black steed, her squeals and giggles piercing the heavy air. For his part, Lord Griffith seemed to enjoy himself as much as his passenger.

The man had a way with children. Maeve had become instantly smitten and stuck to his side. It had been a welcome reprieve, allowing Helen time to organize her thoughts. How could she avoid Scotland and the wedding? One look from her mother and Helen would burst into tears. Even if she didn't, the older Maeve would know immediately something was amiss with her daughter. She always did.

They would make London today and stay in the townhouse. Gideon had notified the staff to be on the ready. Then another two days before they were home. She wanted to hide there and never leave. How could she avoid the wedding?

Helen was not a person to keep emotions at bay. Holding in her grief, her anger, felt like standing in a storm, her emotions battering at her, demanding her attention. It made her tense and grumpy. She'd already snapped at Maeve twice. Her daughter had burst into tears, unused to her mother's sharpness.

I will get through this. The sun will shine again. Her father's words echoed in her brain. Whenever she'd been disappointed, scraped an elbow, or broke a toy—anything that caused tears—her father would lift her onto his knee, wipe her cheeks with his thumbs and tell her, "The sun will shine again, my sweet girl."

And she still believed his words.

London, Mayfair

Helen smelled London before she saw it. The carriage followed the muddy Thames, and the clamor, odors, and ever-present fog reminded her of shopping trips in Town. Street lamps from the row houses beckoned cheerfully as they pulled in front of Number 18 in Grosvenor Square. The familiar front portico with its carved plaster pineapple above the door made her smile. They were putting the past behind them.

The butler opened the door, casting a golden glow on the veranda. Mr. Clarence hadn't changed a bit. Tall and stately, more gray on his balding pate. Maeve had joined her in the carriage and now slept on Helen's lap. A suspicious dark spot appeared on Helen's bodice, near her daughter's open mouth.

"My lady, would you like me to carry Miss Maeve for you?"

She nodded. "Thank you. I don't think she'll sleep long, though."

Lord Griffith reached in and pulled Maeve out of the coach and against his chest. Helen wondered at how natural he looked holding her child. He was a dear man.

"Lady Helen," said Clarence as they walked through the entrance. "It is good to see you again." His words were warm as he bowed, though his face remained stoic.

The housekeeper bobbed a curtsy. Her ruddy cheeks plumped as she smiled and pushed up the silver lock that escaped her cap. "There is a cold supper waiting for you after you are refreshed from your journey. Unless you'd like Cook to make something hot?"

"No, Mrs. Adams, that won't be necessary." Helen tipped her head at the servants, resisting the urge to hug them both and tell them how much she appreciated their hard work. After four years of fending for herself, she saw their roles with different eyes. She'd never take someone for granted again because of their station. "This is Lord Griffith, a friend of Lord Stanfeld. He is our escort back to the estate."

They both nodded their understanding and mumbled a greeting to the earl still holding Maeve. "The snoring lump he's holding is my daughter, Maeve."

Mrs. Adams beamed at her. "After your mother, then?"

"Yes, after my mother." With that simple question and response, Helen was on the verge of tears again.

She turned toward the stairs on the right, blinking rapidly as she ascended. To Helen's surprise, Maeve had not stirred. "We'll lay her down in my room. Do you mind carrying her upstairs?"

"Of course not," he said, shifting the drooling toddler on his shoulder.

They passed the first floor where Helen had entertained friends and played the pianoforte. The second floor held the bedroom for the "children" and hers was the second on the left. She took a deep breath before opening the door. This was the room she had shared with her sister Lottie when they visited London.

It was like stepping back in time. The primrose counterpane with tiny embroidered apples, the thick carpet in a Turkish design of browns, yellow, and greens, and the matching striped wallpaper all brought forth a flood of memories. Her favorite books still sat on the bedside table, the spines of *Swiss Family Robinson* and *Sense and Sensibility* facing out. Mrs. Adams was a saint.

Helen's cheek burned as she pointed toward the bed and watched Lord Griffith lay Maeve on the mattress. The child snuffled against the pillow and curled her body around the rag doll. The earl gently pulled a lock of hair from her mouth. Then he looked up at Helen, back at the bed, and stammered, "I-I will leave you to your rest. What time would you like me to return in the morning?"

"You're staying at a hotel?"

"Actually, your brother set me up in a private club on St. James. The only qualifications are being sponsored by a present or past member and not being married." He moved toward the door. "Anything I need will be provided there. Shall we get another early start?"

"Yes, please." She hesitated, then called to him as he left the room. "Lord Griffith, are you sure wouldn't like to dine here? I realize it's only a cold supper—"

"Yes." He grinned, looking a bit sheepish at his quick acceptance. "I mean, it sounds perfect. With the heat, I couldn't eat a hot meal."

"I'll see you in the parlor, then. It's small but one of my favorite rooms."

As soon as his footsteps faded, she shut the door and opened the wardrobe, praying there was something left behind. With a thank you to the heavens, she pulled out the gray traveling dress. There was a matching spencer, bonnet, and—*thank you, Lord*—a pair of boots. She and Lottie had been the same size when she left.

Helen stripped down to her chemise and pulled on the gown. It was as close to mourning as she could get for now. A pang in her chest reminded her that no one knew, anyway. Her reflection in the Cheval mirror shocked her. For the past four years, she'd avoided her reflection except to ensure a clean face if she were going out. She had not cared about a full-length mirror when she wore such serviceable clothes. Helen studied herself in stunned silence, realizing the toll life in Dublin had taken. The dress hung on her, a once curvy form now thin and flat. Her hair was limp, her eyes dull, and her skin pale. Worst of all, she looked older. Much older than her twenty years. *Don't be vain, you ninny.* Still, she wondered how much weight she'd lost. Her family would see the change before the greetings and hugs had finished.

Mrs. Adams knocked on the door and poked her head in. "May I help you with anything, my lady?"

"Oh, yes. Could you get the buttons and tie the ribbon, please?"

Mrs. Adams clucked as she nimbly finished dressing Helen. "Did you not bring a trunk with you, Lady Helen, er, Mrs. O'Neill?"

"There was a mistake… and my luggage was sent on to our country home."

"I see. Well, this will do in a pinch. The sash will pull in the material enough, so it won't be too bad." She smoothed out Helen's sleeves. "There you go. Sarah will fetch the dirty clothes and have them cleaned before morning."

The housekeeper knew something wasn't right. She'd seen Mrs. Adams's expression when unpacking the bag and small trunk. Servants' clothes. What must she think? *Not now. Don't think of it now.*

"Thank you so much." Helen walked to the bed and lightly rubbed her daughter's back. "She's had quite the time this past week. I wish I had her resilience."

"Children are surely more adaptable than adults. Would you like me to stay with little Maeve, my lady? So, she's not alone if she wakes?"

"Oh, Mrs. Adams, you are a godsend. It would put my mind at ease. I promise I won't be long." She clenched her fists and resisted the urge to hug the older woman. The housekeeper would wonder if Helen had been drinking.

That wasn't a terrible idea.

CHAPTER SIX

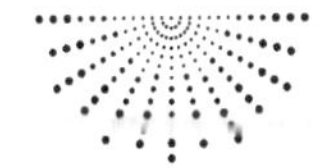

Conway silently cursed himself as he descended the stairs. He was like a schoolboy, gushing at an invitation from the most beautiful girl in the nearby village. She was married. Why did he feel so drawn to her?

It was the sadness in her gaze she tried to hide, perhaps. He longed to make her laugh and show him the side Lord Stanfeld had spoken of. He no longer thought it was fatigue from the trip. He'd seen that look darken in his mother's eyes when his stepfather had been paralyzed and had given up on living. When she had lost the love of her life somewhere in the declining body that she washed and dressed each day.

Could there be a problem in Lady Helen's marriage? Impossible. How could a man not appreciate her beauty and breeding? Something else must have happened. The loss of a friend or even a miscarriage. Well, he'd treat her with care, and if she wished to unburden herself, he would be a sympathetic ear. That was a skill many men had not developed. Conway had learned that some women didn't think him tongue-tied or green, but thoughtful and attentive since he let them babble to their heart's content.

He pulled at his cravat, tugged his fawn waistcoat over his matching trousers, then pulled his sleeves taut beneath his umber tailcoat. Now that they were in Town, he had to dress for dinner or appear uncouth. Though, he still wondered at Lady Helen's wardrobe so far. She seemed to have mixed her luggage up with her maid's. Plain, sturdy clothes that a working-class woman would wear. Conway had not mentioned it; he didn't want to embarrass her.

The parlor was small but well-appointed. Polished walnut paneling, cream curtains, and an Axminster rug made the room cozy. He sat in a chair by the hearth, and the butler appeared with a decanter.

"Sherry before dinner, my lord?" he asked.

"Yes, er, Clarence, isn't it?"

"Yes, my lord," he said with a half bow and handed Conway a cut-crystal glass filled with the ruby liquid. "Thank you, my lord." Another bow and he left the room.

Lady Helen appeared at the door, looking better than he'd seen her since their meeting at the dock. She wore a dove-gray dress with delicate lace at the throat and sleeves. A matching lace ribbon was tied high across the bodice. Her hair shone from a good brushing and was pulled up in an informal bun, curls trailing down to her neck.

"I see your luggage must have beat us to London. You look lovely, Mrs. O'Neill." He stood to greet her properly. "That's no easy feat considering your voyage and the long days we've had on the road."

The corners of her mouth turned up as if she appreciated the compliment. "I must thank you again for all your assistance. You've been more valuable than you can imagine. Especially with Maeve."

"I take it she's in slumberland, then?"

"Yes, it sounded like she was scolding someone in that

place." She led him to the table, and he could smell the mixed scent of vanilla and jasmine she wore. He held out her chair, then sat opposite of her. "She began talking in her sleep as soon as she learned a few words."

"She converses quite well for her age." He'd been impressed with the toddler's speech.

"Unfortunately, there were no children nearby to play with, so it was mostly me and other adults for company." She took a deep breath as if preparing herself for something. "Shall we eat?"

"Certainly. But will she be frightened waking up alone in a strange place?" The thought of Maeve being frightened or crying squeezed his heart.

"How considerate you are, truly," Lady Helen replied, giving him a thoughtful look. Strain showed in the lines around her eyes and mouth, but the sincere smile she bestowed upon him brightened her face. "Mrs. Adams offered to stay with her for just that reason."

A cold salad of thinly sliced veal marinated in oil, vinegar, shallots, and anchovies had been laid out on the table near the window. Warm bread with apricot preserves and butter, thick slices of cheese, and early strawberries finished off the meal.

"I told Mrs. Adams that we would not need anyone to serve us if she set it all out. Do you mind?" she asked, pouring some wine into a glass. She held out the carafe with one copper eyebrow raised. When he picked up his own glass, she filled it.

"I'm a simple man and happy to have a meal with good company." He held up his glass. "To new friends and safe journeys."

Lady Helen held up her own glass, a slight twinkle in her blue eyes. "Agreed. Though I somehow doubt you are a simple man, Lord Griffith. And I can guarantee company, though perhaps not good."

Conway served them each some of the beef, then picked up his fork. He watched her put a bite in her mouth and close her eyes as she chewed. Either this was her favorite dish, and she savored it, or she hadn't had it in a long time. Again, that voice in his head told him something was not quite right.

"Tell me, what is life like in Ireland? Did you live in the city or did you have a country home?"

She blanched, and he thought she might be ill. Or had their place of residence been a sore spot between her and her husband? Slowly, she finished chewing, then swallowed. "We preferred the city of Dublin."

"I see. I assume there were more amusements for the family."

Lady Helen nodded and began slathering a hunk of bread with butter, then spooned honey onto it.

Conway racked his brain for more conversation. "We've been fortunate with the weather, don't you think?"

"It's unbearably hot." Lady Helen paused, the bread almost to her mouth. When she looked at him, those deep blue pools made his heart beat faster. With a sigh and a softening around her mouth, she said, "I apologize. You're right. We've been very lucky there has been no rain to slow us down. And there were no privateers on the Irish Sea or heavy storms."

He grinned. "That's the spirit. Always a bright side to everything, my mother always says."

"Is your mother here in England?" she asked, studying her bread once again.

"No, she lives with my younger brother and his wife in Wales. It's a couple of days' ride from my estate." Conway finished his beef and added more to his plate. It was very tender and expertly seasoned. "I wondered how Doc's new wife would get along in our wild country, coming from London, but Evie seems happy wherever Brecken is. And she charmed my mother as she does everyone."

"You like your sister-in-law, then?"

He nodded. "She's a prize, to be sure."

"Your brother… is a physician?"

Conway laughed. "No, though he doctored enough animals as a youth. His name is Madoc—Doc is our family nickname—and he holds the title Earl of Brecken. Do you get along well with your husband's family?"

Another pause before she spoke, "He had none. I suppose that could be a blessing for some, but I enjoy family."

"Something we have in common." Conway reached for the bread and sopped up the leftover gravy from the plate.

"Are you married, Lord Griffith?"

He shook his head, that emptiness creeping into his belly again. "Not yet, though it's about time I thought about it."

"You're not afraid of the leg shackles?"

"I'm not. My mother and my father—stepfather, my own father dying before I was born—had a marriage full of love and laughter. It is proof that it can be a happy institution."

"He raised you?" she asked, reaching for a strawberry.

Conway frowned at the meat still on her plate. He'd had the impression she enjoyed the dish, but she'd eaten only a few bites, a small chunk of bread, and now moved on to the fruit. No wonder she was so thin. "He did. Taught me everything I needed to know to be a good landlord, a good person, I hope."

"So, if your father died before you were born, and your brother is younger, then he is your half brother. Are you close?"

"We are the best of friends. I would trust him with my

life." He watched her put the berry to her mouth and take a delicate bite with small white teeth. The bright red against the pink of her lips… *Blast* if he didn't have a sudden craving for a strawberry.

"That is high praise, indeed." She smiled and stood. "If you'll excuse me, I should get back upstairs to my daughter. She's in capable hands, but Mrs. Adams is still a stranger should Maeve wake. I'll bid you good night."

"I thought we would leave at first light, so we can stop earlier and avoid the deuced heat." He also stood and followed her to the hall. "Would that suit you?"

"That sounds perfect. I'm sure Maeve will wake early after so many hours of sleep."

He watched her ascend the stairs and almost jumped when Clarence cleared his throat from behind. "God's teeth, man, you're as stealthy as a thief in the night."

"Thank you, my lord." He gave a small bow and held out Conway's hat. "Will you be taking the carriage or your horse?"

"My horse, I think. It's a clear night."

"I thought so. It has been saddled and is waiting for you." The butler walked around him and opened the door.

"Are you always this proficient at knowing what is needed and when?" Conway asked, amused.

"I endeavor to ensure all things run smoothly, my lord."

Conway jogged down the stairs and took the reins from the waiting stable boy. Granted, they weren't far from the mews, but it was still impressive. Not even time moved that fast in Wales. Mounting his horse, he proceeded toward St. James with a whistle on his lips.

"Whoa," he murmured as he stopped the gelding in front of an inconspicuous building in an inconspicuous neighborhood.

A single **W** hung above the door of the Wicked Earls'

Club. He'd laughed at the moniker until seeing the interior. The owner had told him to ask Charles for anything he might need. Charles, a short round man with a blank face, had already secured Conway a room for the night and a bottle of French brandy awaited him. The membership fee was staggering, but the benefits were superb. An exclusive floor of this club, a set of private rooms for each member, and almost any vice for the asking. It might be worth the blunt to pay for a membership if he were to return to London for an extended stay.

The downstairs of the establishment resembled any other gentlemen's club. There were rooms for gaming, a library for those who preferred quieter entertainment or conversation, and a dining room. He followed the sound of masculine shouts to a crowded gaming room. A small group of men were engaged in conversation near a fireplace. Several tables flanked the right side of the room where various games of whist, faro, and hazard were in progress. Indeed, this could be a comfortable residence the next time he was in Town.

His footsteps were muffled on the luxurious wool carpet that lined the back stairs. Polished mahogany shone from the wall lamps as he turned down the hall of private rooms.

The first door was open, and he poked his head in. It was a billiard room, rectangular and well-appointed with the table at the far end. Its golden, scrolled legs gleamed in the firelight, ending in lion heads under each of the corner pockets. In front of him, chairs were arranged facing a larger table in a semicircle, presumably for cards. Behind it was a side table and two decanters. By the colors of the liquid, he guessed one to be port and the other brandy. Gleaming linenfold paneling of French walnut surrounded all four sides with Axminster carpet underfoot.

Decadent was the word that came to mind. Not his style of course, but for an occasional indulgence… why not? He'd been told he could request anything with a tug on a rope. He stared at that bellpull now as he sat on his bed. A bed with multiple feather ticks and satin bed linens. But what would he possibly ask for?

A vision of Lady Helen eating a strawberry filled his head as he lay back with a groan.

CHAPTER SEVEN

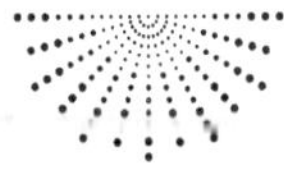

Two days later
Stanfeld Estate, Norfolk Count

Y

The first sight of Stanfeld Manor brought tears to her eyes.

The carriage stopped at a crossroads, letting a mail coach go through. Helen popped her head out of the window and saw it, proud and majestic upon the distant hill. As they drew closer, she fought to keep the sobs at bay. They would be safe. They were home. *Home.*

The numerous windows of the imposing, three-story, medieval manor glinted and flashed like jewels in a crown of gray sandstone. The steep gables seemed to stand sentry, and the four corners of the manor were miniature turrets that looked like arrows pointing to the heavens. Surrounded by the original moat, it reminded visitors of long-gone knights, fair maidens, and chivalry.

She'd been so impatient to leave this place. Once gone, she'd dreamt of returning—not just to the estate—but to the atmosphere of happy, shared memories and love. The grounds of Stanfeld had always been full of love.

The carriage rolled to a stop. Maeve waved to her from her favorite place, sitting in front of the earl on his horse. The driver lifted her daughter to the ground before Lord Griffith dismounted, then lowered the steps for Maeve to exit the vehicle. As her own feet hit the cobblestones, a blur of brown and white came around one side of the house, yipping furiously. Its tail wagged faster than a hawk moth's wings sipping at honeysuckle.

"Little Bit!" she cried, bending low to catch the small dog as it jumped at her. The dog slurped her cheek with his tongue and barked some more. Helen buried her face in the wiry fur and breathed in the smell of the stable. Then Little Bit turned his attention to the human who was more his size.

"A puppy, Mama. You not tell me we had a puppy."

"Isn't it a wonderful surprise?" asked Lord Griffith, squatting and giving the terrier a scratch behind its ears. "I have a few of my own."

Walking with Maeve's hand in hers, they made their way up the portico steps just as the great oak doors opened wide.

There was Sanders, looking just as old as he always had. His gray eyes twinkled as he bowed to their party. "Lady Helen, you have been missed," he said simply.

Without thought, she hugged the man. He was the closest thing to family that she'd seen in four years. He patted her awkwardly on the back, turned red as a ripe apple, then faced Maeve. "And is this Lady Stanfeld's namesake?" he asked, covering his embarrassment.

"It is. I cannot wait to show her the grounds." Helen led

the way into the hall and sucked in her breath. She pointed to the portraits lining the walls. "These are your family, my sweet."

But Maeve walked straight to the suit of armor standing guard in the entryway, next to the circular staircase. Knocking on the metal, she put her ear to it.

"Who's in heeah?" she asked, now sticking an eye against one of the slats in the armor.

Lord Griffith chuckled. "I think your mother meant the paintings up there." He pointed, and she followed the direction of his finger.

"Oh. They look mad." She put her hands on her hips, furrowed her brows, and pursed her lips. "Do I look like them?"

"A mirror reflection to be sure," said the earl.

The small form of the housekeeper, Mrs. Laskey, came bustling down the hall, her frizzed orange curls barely contained by her cap. "Oh, my lady, it's so good to see you." Unlike the butler, she welcomed the unexpected hug from Helen. "This house hasn't been the same since you snuck away. And this is your precious daughter?"

"My name is Maeve Chahlotte—that is my aunt—O'Neill," she said with a wobbly curtsy. "It is vewy good to meet you, my lady."

"Such fine manners," cooed the housekeeper. "But I'm afraid I'm only Mrs. Laskey, not my lady."

Helen made the introductions and explained that Lord Griffith would be staying the night. Her hands were trembling by the time she reached her old bedchamber. Maeve followed her in, jumping onto the sunny counterpane and reaching for the canopy above. The tiny pink and yellow roses lining the cream wallpaper were cheery and still made her smile. Her favorite color had always been yellow. She'd picked the color when she'd been old enough to choose. The color had echoed her optimistic disposition. *I surround myself with somber tones these days,* she thought, looking down at her gray traveling dress and pulling off her bonnet.

Then she watched her daughter leap off the bed and run for the window seat, squealing when she saw the garden. "Mama, I wanna see the flowahs. So many of them, see?"

"Yes, my sweet. But first, we must wash off the dust from the road—"

"We took a bath in London. I don't want anothah."

"We will wash off the dust, change our clothes, and then get some refreshment. After that"—Helen wagged her finger as Maeve opened her mouth to protest—"we will walk in the garden. I have many things to show you here at Stanfeld."

"Hot water is on the way, my lady," added Mrs. Laskey. "It will only take three shakes of a lamb's tail, and the little miss will have her wish. What time did you want dinner?"

When was the last time someone had asked her that?

"Since it's already late afternoon, and we'll have tea shortly, why don't we say eight o'clock? Would that be too late for Cook?" Helen bit the inside of her lip when the housekeeper gave her a strange look.

"Whatever time you prefer, my lady, will suit Cook."

"Yes, then eight, please."

It was dream-like being home again, dressing for dinner in her old clothes she'd left behind. Though, they would all need to be taken in. Her family would be appalled by her weight loss.

Thank you, Mama. Guilt nipped at Helen as she surveyed the indigo dress with Vandyke lace edging on the modest bodice, sleeves, and hem. It was really a winter shade, but she had little choice. It was the closest color she had for mourning, without telling anyone she was in mourning. Since she'd arrived on the Stanfeld grounds, her need to fall apart and fill the nearby pond with tears had diminished. Something about being in this familiar place gave her comfort and strength. Everything would be fine now.

The sun will shine again. "I miss you, Papa," she whispered to the ceiling. "I wish you could have known your granddaughter."

Mrs. Laskey appeared at the door with Maeve, dressed in a lovely pale-pink gown that stopped just below her knees. "She insisted on this one, my lady. It's a bit small, but we managed. And she ate enough for two."

"Tawts, Mama. With bewies inside and icing on top. And fat, gween peas." Maeve patted her belly. "I'm this full." And she held out her arms.

"Thank you, Mrs. Laskey. I've decided we'll be staying in England indefinitely. Is there still a seamstress in the village?"

"Yes, my lady. And her daughter is working for her now too."

"Could you arrange to have them come to Stanfeld? I'll need a new wardrobe for Maeve and a few things for myself." She bent to tweak her daughter's nose. "Would you like to choose the colors for your new clothes?"

"And Ahwohwah too?"

"I suppose Aurora may have a new dress," Helen agreed as she took the tiny plump hand. "Let us get some tea."

They met Lord Griffith on the first-floor landing, also on his way to the drawing room. "Perfect timing," he declared. "Aren't you the loveliest ladies on the estate? I am a very lucky man."

"And then we go to the gawden." She held up her arms, and Lord Griffith swung her into the air.

"I see my daughter has charmed you as well," Helen said with a chuckle.

"I believe I was easy prey. Now, your butler will be a more severe test." His voice was light with amusement. "However, I did hear *someone* asking him about good hiding places."

"Sandews knows the vewy best places. Mama will never win when we play hide-and-seek." Her smug smile had both adults chuckling.

After tea and the most delicious biscuits Helen had eaten in years, they strolled in the garden. Lord Griffith smelled of spiced bergamot, and Helen found she liked the scent. While she and the earl walked, Maeve ran, skipped, somersaulted, hopped on one leg, and named every color of flower she passed.

"I wish I had half her energy."

Helen studied the earl's profile as he observed her daughter. He was taller than her but not of great height; his body was muscled and solid as a tree trunk. His shoulders filled out the forest-green waistcoat, and the matching trousers hugged his muscular thighs. Thick dark hair, combed back and partially tamed, shone black with threads of blue in the fading sun. A lock would break loose from the pomade's hold on occasion, and he'd push it back impatiently. A square jaw, tanned skin that told her he enjoyed the outdoors, and dark eyes that glittered like a shard of cold obsidian.

Then he turned his gaze on her, and she marveled at the warmth she saw there. "It's a lovely garden. Did you spend much time here as a girl?"

She nodded. "Here, the stable, and Lake Perfect were my favorite haunts."

He grinned. "Lake Perfect? I should have high expectations, then?"

They'd reach the outskirts of the garden, with hawthorn trees guarding the delicate plants from hungry animals and heavy winds. Maeve waved at them from under one of the trees, jumping to catch a low-hanging branch.

"Careful of the thorns," he called. The girl quit hopping and glared at the branches, looking for the offensive spikes. "She doesn't stop until she sleeps, eh?"

"Indeed." Helen smiled, feeling lighter than she had in weeks. No, years. Her heart ached, but it also told her she was where she needed to be.

"Now, about Lake Perfect," prompted the earl.

"Ah, it's actually a small pond."

"Already the name implies embellishment." He winked at her, and a rush of heat flooded her belly.

"I was a little girl and thought it was an enormous body of water. It provided fish for my brother's favorite pastime, swimming during the summer heat, and ice skating in the winter. I used to sit under a tree at one end and talk to the squirrels. I imagined being friends with all the creatures in the forest, insisting to my family that I shared a common language with the animals."

"Did you?"

The question surprised her. She looked up to see a mischievous twinkle in his dark eyes. He was teasing her! "I will admit to several long conversations with some bullfrogs. The squirrels liked my imitation of their chatter enough to talk back once in a while."

"It sounds enchanting."

Helen laughed. It was a strange sound coming from her throat, but it slid up and out. When had she last done that? She couldn't remember. "I was always told I had a vivid imagination."

As the sun dipped behind the hawthorns, Maeve skipped back to them. She tried to hide a yawn behind her fist, but the fatigue showed in her eyes. "It's time for my sweet girl to say good night. Tomorrow will be another day filled with new sights and sounds."

Maeve nodded her head and again raised her arms to

Lord Griffith. Helen swallowed the sadness as she watched her daughter carried by another man. How would she tell Maeve about her own papa? How would she feel about growing up without a proper father? With a deep breath, she put the questions from her mind. There was time to figure it out. Her family would help her find the words.

Or would they urge her to take another husband in the future? Helen shuddered at the thought. Love had caused her nothing but pain. She'd prefer to avoid pain if she could. Widowhood was much more appealing to her at this point. Yet shame filled her as she listened to Maeve's giggle when the earl tossed her in the air and caught her. Didn't her daughter deserve someone like Lord Griffith to adore and spoil her?

CHAPTER EIGHT

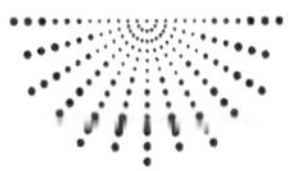

Conway was glad to see Lady Helen eat with more gusto. *Relish might be a better word,* he thought as she closed her eyes on the next bite of poached sole. Being home seemed to improve her color too. Perhaps she was prone to seasickness, and the voyage had been hard on her. Regardless, he welcomed the change.

He took a sip of wine and brought up the subject he'd been dreading. "I believe I shall begin my journey home tomorrow."

Her fork froze midway to her mouth. When her gaze clashed with his, he saw disappointment. Why did that make his pulse dance? Did she enjoy his company? *It doesn't matter, you blunderhead.*

"Of course. You have been more than generous with your time." She smiled. "I do hope we meet again."

"If you lived here, I would be certain of it. But I rarely visit Ireland, so the odds are against it." It sounded so final.

"We shall leave it to fate, then." Lady Helen's eyes grew wide as a servant entered with a steaming dish of custard, a pitcher of cream, and fresh berries. "My favorite."

"Fate?" he asked with a grin.

She laughed, a sweet sound that seemed to match the pudding.

"You are a goose. Mrs. Laskey remembered how I love custard." She sighed and picked up a spoon. "I can smell the nutmeg. How I've missed some of these spices."

"There is a shortage of spices in Dublin, Mrs. O'Neill?" He wished he hadn't asked when her smile crumbled. Was it a coincidence or did her mood change any time she was asked about Ireland? By this time, he wondered if she disliked the place.

"Um, a few of my particular favorites." She dished the custard into a small bowl, poured a dollop of warm cream on top, and added a spoonful of berries. Her expression lightened. "Do you care for it, my lord?"

"I do, though I have a feeling your cook must make it exceptionally well." And once he had a bite, he had to agree with Lady Helen. It melted in his mouth.

"I believe I'm in heaven," she mumbled around another bite. "How I missed this."

After they finished, he asked, "Would you like to take another stroll in the garden? Or play Whist?"

She pursed her lips in thought. Conway imagined kissing them, soft and still sweet from the custard. "I would prefer to visit the stable. Hopefully, my pony is still there."

"To the stable, it is," he agreed, pushing away from the table.

Lady Helen was at home with the horses. Little Bit followed them, yapping at her skirts. She stopped twice to scratch behind the dog's ears. As they passed each stall, Lady Helen named every horse. "Here is my Frog," she said, stopping in front of a little bay mare. It had four white stockings and a blaze on its forehead. The horse snorted and let out a soft nicker. "I didn't forget."

She held out a piece of carrot, then turned to the next stall with a frown.

"Don't tell me there is an animal you don't like?"

"No, of course not! I don't recognize him. Gideon must have bought him after I left."

"*That* is Verity. He bought the beast at Tattersalls when he was told it was untrainable." Conway reached up and rubbed the horse's soft black neck. "Your brother believed he'd only been trained badly and obviously beaten. He had welts all over him at the time. It took months, but Stanfeld made him into a deuced good horse."

"Verity. Truth. Sounds like Gideon."

Lady Helen turned back to her own mare and fed her another bite of carrot. "I will see you tomorrow, Frog." She kissed the horse on the nose and turned to leave.

"I have to ask," he said, stopping her with a hand on her arm. "Why Frog?"

She laughed, her cheeks pink. "When she was a foal, she would hop around the pasture, and I thought she looked like a dark furry frog. In my defense, I was only five."

Conway snorted. "You poor thing," he told the pretty mare, admiring her shiny deep brown fur. "I would have given you a more prestigious name, like Hoppy or Bunny."

"Ha! In some cultures, the frog represents wealth and abundance. So, I find my name to be quite as respectable as your silly monikers." She gave him a mock glare and ambled toward the door.

"I concede, my lady," he said with a formal bow, enjoying her newfound spirit.

Just outside the stable, she sat on a bench next to the door. He joined her and realized she was watching the last remnants of the sunset. "It's beautiful, isn't it?"

"Yes. There is something about a sunrise or sunset in the country. It's not the same in a city with buildings blocking the view." She sighed and leaned her head against the building. "And the birdsong can't be heard over all the noise. The trill of the wren at dawn or the song thrush in the evening."

"I'm beginning to think you are more of a country girl. Ladies who appreciate the sedate joys of rural life are rare." He thought of the women who had tried to interest him in marriage in the past. None would have been happy with an occasional trip to London. Life at Gruffyd Estate would have been intolerably dull for them.

"Honestly, I didn't realize what I preferred until I left. As a sixteen-year-old scholar of life, I forged ahead without thought. I knew so much more than my parents."

"It didn't seem to turn out too badly, though," Conway said, giving her a slight elbow. "Maeve is quite the treasure."

"She is."

"So, will you be leaving shortly for Scotland? The wedding is early August if memory serves me well. I'd estimate a good week or more for travel."

"Yes, I—no, I mean…" She stood, her hands clenched in front of her, her bottom lip trembling. "I'm not sure if I will go."

"Why? Are you concerned for your daughter? Is it too long of a journey after coming from Dublin?" Even in the evening light, he could see how she had paled. But she only shook her head.

"Mrs. O'Neill, I can't help but see you are distraught whenever I bring up certain subjects. Is there anything I can do?" He wrapped his fingers around her slim arm and turned her to face him. Conway couldn't stand the sadness and fear in her sparkling eyes. What could she possibly be afraid of? "Please, let me help you—"

"He's dead!" she cried out. "I came alone because he's dead." Her hands covered her face, and she began to sob. Great heaving sobs that shook her narrow shoulders.

Without thought, he pulled her close, rubbing her back and rocking them back and forth. "Shhh, now. It will be fine. Everything will be fine." The sobs continued, and he maintained his hold, absorbing her tremors into his own body and giving comfort.

"How?"

A hiccup and a sniffle. He pulled out his handkerchief and handed it to her. She dabbed at her eyes and blew her nose, then looked up at him with red splotches covering her cheeks. "Shot and killed during a skirmish. His first love was Ireland and its politics, fighting for the rights of the people. He worked for Daniel O'Connell."

"Ah." It was making sense now. O'Connell was a loud voice in Ireland's struggle for rights within the United Kingdom. But he'd killed a man and had since avoided conflict. "But I heard that after two duels, he swore to remain peaceful. He's been adamant about ignoring insults and proud about his refusals to fight."

"He may turn a deaf ear to the jeers, but his men do not. I learned of Rory's death in the middle of the night, torn from my bed, and forced to flee. His friends feared the constable would seek to make an example of my husband by punishing his family." Her eyes darkened with more tears. "I packed what I could, sent a letter off to Gideon, and fled with Maeve like a coward."

The sobs began again, and Conway cradled her in his arms once more. He closed his eyes as the warmth of her body seeped into his, feeling her slight curves fit against his perfectly. The momentary joy of hearing she was a widow had been drowned out by her sobs and confession. How had she kept this to herself for so long?

"Your family doesn't know?"

Her head moved against his chest, and she looked into his

eyes. "They believe I am living a respectable life, married to a wealthy squire."

"But in truth?"

"A two-room apartment on the third floor in a shabby part of Dublin. It was easy to lie to Mama in letters. But now…" With a sigh, she pushed against his chest and stepped away.

He resisted the urge to take her hand and bring her closer. "Now your family will take one look at you and know something is wrong."

She nodded and blew her nose again. With a deep steadying breath, Lady Helen told him the sad story. She'd been duped, led away from friends and family, and isolated in a new place. He wanted to strangle the man, except he was already dead. Yet, she must have loved him to stay.

"Well, we'll have to find a way to provide the time you need to face them," he said once she'd finished.

"How?"

Conway did take her hand this time, slid it onto his arm, and guided them back toward the house. "I'm quite sure Maeve had a sniffle this evening before bed. By morning, I fear she may not be able to travel."

Lady Helen peeked up at him beneath her wet lashes. "Nothing serious, of course. Just not well enough to make the journey. We will look forward to congratulating the happy couple in person when they return to Stanfeld." She blew out a loud relieved sigh.

"I believe you have your letter half written."

"And I believe you are my hero."

CHAPTER NINE

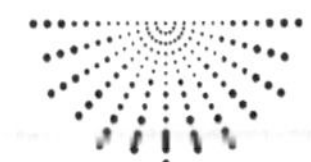

Horrified and heartened and oh, so relieved. Opposite words that described the conflicting emotions swirling within her. Horrified that she had spilled her secrets to a man she barely knew. Heartened that his reaction had not been to turn away from her or be disgusted by her lies. And relieved to be able to share her secret finally. She wanted to throw her arms around this man and tell him how very, very much she appreciated him.

"I cannot imagine bearing such a burden alone. This does provide the missing pieces to the puzzle." Lord Griffith had escorted her inside, and they were stopped at the foot of the stairs. "You have hardly resembled Gideon's description of you."

"I can imagine some of the things he's told you."

"None of them included a quiet, staid woman. But you are not yourself under the circumstances." He lifted his hand, his fingers curled as if he might brush her cheek, then dropped it to his side. "It seems we've quite traded roles."

"How so?" He was such a kind man. She would have to

thank Gideon once her tale had been told to the entire family.

"I am usually the quiet one, especially in female company, that is. I'm terrible with polite conversation, never had much practice or use for it. So, the ladies considered me dull or uninterested. Those that pursued me were after my wealth." He shrugged, and his face turned a trace of red. "Now we've both shared a secret."

"You've not had any difficulty conversing with me."

"No, I have not. I assumed it was because you were married. I've always been more comfortable with females that are already spoken for or related to me."

She laughed. "I'm certainly not related to you. Will you lose your tongue now that you know I'm widowed?"

The smile slid from his face. "No. I will always be happy—er, comfortable around you. I felt a kinship with you the first time I looked at your cameo image."

Why did her heart suddenly beat so? The longing on the man's face was undeniable. *He wants you.* Panic throbbed in her belly. Would he try to kiss her, take advantage of her as another had done? Loving a man had been like living inside a tempest, wrenching her into its center, taking her breath away for moments at a time, then drowning her heart in doubt and regret.

"Thank you for sharing a piece of your life with me, Mrs. O'Neill." He bowed and gave her a wide smile. "It has been a memorable adventure. I only wish we could have met under better circumstances."

"Perhaps one day, we shall." No, her instinct had been right. He was a good man.

"I must say I'm worried for you, though. Would it help if I stayed longer? I have no pressing commitments and could easily delay my return by a week."

Helen shook her head. "No, though I thank you for your

concern and all you've done for me and Maeve. Lending an ear to my troubles has been a tremendous boon to my spirits."

He gave her another bow and kissed the back of her hand. "I consider you and your daughter my friends. May I write and see how you both fare?"

A small smile turned up her lips. "I should like that, Lord Griffith. I should like that very much."

❦

The next morning was bittersweet. The sun shone, and the sky was a cloudless blue. Maeve was in high spirits, but pouting that her friend had to leave. Just as the tears were starting, Little Bit saved the day. The terrier came wagging up to his new charge, tugging on the hem of her dress with his teeth. The peal of giggles was instant, and off she went, chasing the dog.

"I'm so easily replaced," cried Lord Griffith, his hand at his chest. "Beware the fickle female."

"Not all of us are so easily distracted, my lord."

"No." He turned to her, the rein in his hand. His driver had left with the coach already, knowing his lord would catch up easily on horseback. "I need you to promise me something." His tone was serious, and he caught her in a direct gaze.

"Yes?"

"If you need anything—*anything*—do not hesitate to write. I've given you my address." He mounted his horse, swinging his powerful leg over the saddle, and tipped his hat. "Do I have your word?"

"On my honor!" She placed her hand over her heart. "I swear."

"Then I shall leave you in good conscience, my lady. Until

we meet again."

He gave the horse a light kick with his heels, and it took off in a trot. She watched him all the way down the drive and through the gates, feeling a loss as he disappeared from sight.

Nothing like the present, she thought as she headed to the parlor. She would write a letter and let her family know she would not attend the wedding. It would be mid-August before they returned. That gave her plenty of time to put on some weight and prepare for their reunion. Her words would be calm and practiced by then.

❦

Gruffyd Estate, Wales

The trip home had afforded Conway too much time to think. Lady Helen—which he now called her since she was a widow—was free. In mourning, granted, but free. It had been unsettling news. Of course, he would be smitten with a woman who was complicated. She was mourning a husband she'd loved enough to risk losing her family. And he knew how close Stanfeld was to his sisters.

Time would be an ally. Time would give her balance and perspective, allowing them to become closer through letters. He was in no hurry. Let her grieve the fool who had chosen politics over her. A yell bubbled up inside him and burst from his throat. "YEESSSSS!" His horse perked its ears, sidling back and forth as Conway let out another triumphant shout.

This was a new emotion. The excited anticipation of seeing a woman, *Lady Helen,* again. For he would, he knew without a doubt. If he had to invent some new business deal with Stanfeld, he'd return to England after the New Year. He would begin with friendship and correspondence. Words were much easier to put on paper than to formulate and say in a moment. He could take his time and deliberate each word.

He had gone over all the oddities he'd encountered since they met. The companion sent ahead, practically no luggage, the way she savored the well-cooked meals, the sadness and pain in her deep blue eyes, the silence and distraction. His instincts had been right. Something had been wrong, but he'd had no idea how wrong. Yet she had demonstrated such strength, such courage to keep her daughter safe and reach her destination. Home.

It was something they shared, the love of home and family. He could picture Maeve running in the gardens of Gruffyd, riding one of the ponies to the stream, laughing with her mother while they picnicked on the bank.

Getting ahead of yourself, old man.

It didn't matter. He was a stubborn Welshman. Once he set his mind to something, nothing shy of a herd of raging cattle could stop him. And his mind was set on Lady Helen and her daughter Maeve, for one did not come without the other.

Nor would he want it any other way.

❦

He tossed the reins to the stable boy. "Rub him down good, lad. He's come a long way."

"Yes, milord," said the dark-haired boy, jogging away with the horse.

Conway wanted to wash the road off him and let his grandmother know he had returned. He found her in the library, reading by the window. Her favorite lace shawl, spun

…r thread that matched her hair, lay across her

…, you've made it back to me," she declared.

He noticed she grimaced as she rose from the chair. Her bones were aching more this year, and he worried that winter would be hard on her. "You'd send the devil himself after me if I did not."

She chuckled, her dark eyes still sharp. "Come give this old woman a hug and tell me of your journey."

Conway raised his hands, palms out. "I need a bath, Grandmama. You won't be so happy to see me if you come much closer."

With a chortle, she waved him off. "Go, then. I'll see you in the drawing room before supper. We'll talk and have a glass of wine."

"Grandmama, dinner was excellent," he said, smacking his lips on the last of the mutton stew. "I think I shall retire early tonight. It's been a long day."

"I can imagine. It's good to hear the cattle brought a nice price. You have a head for business that your father never had." She rose from her chair. "Come sit with me by the fire for a bit. I won't be awake much longer, either. My bedtime seems to get earlier every year."

"You should slow down."

"You should marry," she said, wagging a finger at him. "And you won't find any prospects riding with drovers and fetching a friend's married sister."

"About that…" He offered her his arm to help her up the stairs, and they settled themselves in her private sitting room. If there had been guests, she would never have allowed anyone to assist her. Her pride was great, her opinions narrow, and her words often curt, but Conway neve… doubted her love for him.

Once Lady Griffith had a glass of wine in her hand, she turned to Conway. "You said, 'About that' when we were coming upstairs. Continue, please."

He paused, wondering where to start. There was no need to report every detail. "The lady I escorted is not married. She is recently widowed."

"Stanfeld's sister?" She pursed her lips and stared at the fire. "How long has she been widowed?"

"Not long."

"And you like her?"

"I do. She also has a daughter, about three years of age. We got along splendidly."

"She already has a child?" She frowned. "At least it's a girl. No competition once you have an heir."

"I said I liked her, and you have us married with a babe already." He clucked his tongue. "Slow down, Grandmama. I only arrived home a few hours ago. Besides, she loved this man enough to give up her family for him. She may not even be open to a second marriage."

"You've never said you *liked* any woman before. I shall take good news as it comes. The widow aspect, however—when will her mourning be finished?" Her gaze was steady and practical as if she spoke about purchasing a pregnant broodmare. "And what woman with a drop of intelligence and any kind of sense would not want to marry you?"

He snorted. "Plenty, I'm sure. First, I don't know if the lady will be open to my courtship. Second, I believe I will begin with correspondence. She has yet to inform her family of the situation."

"So, you *have* decided. I can read you like my favorite book, Gruff. Tell me your plan, then, for I can see you have one."

CHAPTER TEN

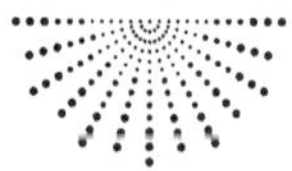

Stanfeld Estate, Norfolk
Mid-August

Helen sighed as she leaned back against the tub. Her hair was washed, the water was still warm, and the fire crackled cheerfully. Her family had taken the news well. Gideon had been outraged. "How dare the man use you for his own gain. To trick you into leaving England. If you'd written to me, I'd have taken care of him."

Her sisters—having extended their trip to see Helen and meet Maeve—were empathetic, of course. They were both married and in love with their husbands but assured Helen that time would heal her heart. "As Papa always said," they chimed in unison, "the sun will shine again." She hadn't mentioned the fact her heart had been broken long before her husband had died.

Her new sister-in-law, Lissie, had only hugged her. A widow when she had met Gideon, Lissie understood the loss and how lacking words could be. Helen had a feeling he new sister would be a sympathetic ear.

Mama had been a bit of both, her red cheeks matching her hair. "That rapscallion! Oh, if I could… But my dear girl, how are you coping? How has little Maeve taken this?"

"I haven't told her." That was the only time her breathing had stopped, and she blinked back the tears. "I don't know how. Will she even understand what 'dead' means?"

"We will think on it," Mama had decided.

A soft rap on the door interrupted her thoughts, and her new lady's maid entered. "Are you finished, my lady?" She was a girl from the nearby village, perhaps eighteen. Her mother was the seamstress and had mentioned her daughter when she came for Helen and Maeve's fitting. Tess was a slender girl with light brown hair, green eyes, and an infectious smile.

"Yes, the water is getting tepid." As Tess wrapped the towel around her, squeezing the wet strands of hair sticking to her back, the maid began to hum. "That sounds like a lullaby I sing to my daughter."

"It is, my lady. Since I've also been helping with Miss Maeve, she taught me the song so I could sing with her at bedtime." Tess held up the night rail and pulled it over her mistress's thin body. "You need to eat more, ma'am. There's nothin' to you."

"I'm trying. And thank you for your help with Maeve. The nurse should arrive by the end of the week, and the nursery will be ready by then too." She looked over at the small form in her bed. "She doesn't even realize what she's been through."

"I don't mind a'toll, my lady. She's a sweet, beautiful little girl. And there's not a contrary bone in her body. Always willing to do whatever she's told and smiling to boot." Tess pushed her mistress toward the hearth, set her in a chair, and

ITH

rying her hair. "Besides, I'm living in this fine so I'm here whenever you need me."

uckled. "Thank you, Tess." It was odd to have someone helping with her bath. *Pff!* It was odd to have a bath whenever she wished. Mama said she would get used to it all again, but she wasn't sure. She was certain that she'd never take a servant for granted again. A kind word, a show of appreciation were simple things to give another person. Something so small could mean so much. Another life lesson, she supposed.

When Tess had gone, Helen went to her side table and pulled out the letter from Lord Griffith. He had been solicitous, asking not only about her but Maeve and hoping all had gone well with her family. He'd also made her laugh with some of his tales about the villagers and the Welsh superstitions that were still prevalent. Some were ridiculous, like spying the first daffodil gives the finder more gold than silver throughout the year. Others could truly be profitable.

A man in the village named Rhun works for the local farmers. He helps bring in crops and delivers the goods once sold. There is an old Welsh saying that the appearance of a load of hay in front of you means that good luck will attend you.

The farmers had gathered at the tavern and were complaining that every time they send Rhun out to deliver a wagonload of hay, it takes him all day. So, they asked the man, "Why can ye manage a load of vegetables by midmorning, but it takes ye till supper for the hay?"

Rhun answered, "I'm a man of good will, ye know. So, I wait along the main road, and when I see someone comin', I pull the wagon in front of them. I like to spread luck amongst my friends and kin whenever I can." He took a puff off his pipe and grinned.

The farmers nodded and chewed on this for a moment. One

said, "But you don't get paid as much if you only deliver the one load of hay in a day. You'll lose money to give people a bit of luck?"

The barkeep leaned in on the conversation. "Oh, he doesn't lose a ha'penny. He finds those friends and kin in here eventually. Somehow, the conversation always turns to the hay, the luck coming their way, and the empty bumper in front of himself."

"Ye ask a man to buy ye a drink after doing him a good deed?" asked one farmer, frowning at Rhun.

"No, now that would be bad manners. I just remind them of my thoughtfulness, and they are always happy to partake in another ale with me. No one wants to cross fate."

"What he loses by not driving an extra load, he makes up for in ale over the next week."

Helen laughed again as she reread it. She missed him, though they had been together for little more than a week. Yet, she'd felt she'd known him so much longer. Her response had not been as lighthearted, relaying her news, but it had ended on a happy note. Gideon had also written a letter of thanks. Her brother had sung Griffith's praises, declaring him a clever businessman and a kind and generous earl.

About the same time in a little pub in Wales...

Lord Griffith ducked under the short door frame and peered around the dim pub. With only two windows facing the east, the place was always darker in the afternoon. A fire crackled at the far end of the no candles or lanterns had been lit yet for the

n, milord, come in," called the barkeep as he a mug with a towel. "What's yer pleasure this fine afternoon?"

Conway spied the man he was looking for, leaning on the end of the bar near the hearth. He moved to join him and ordered a bumper of ale.

"G'day," the man said.

"Good day to you, Rhun," he replied. The barkeep set a pint in front of him, and Conway raised it to the old man. "May I buy your next one?"

Rhun's eyes grew wide, and he pointed to himself. "Me, milord?"

"Aye, it's why I came." Conway pushed more than enough coin to cover both drinks. "I wanted to thank you."

"Me, milord?" the flabbergasted man asked again.

"You." He smiled at the older man's confusion. "Do you remember last month when we had the conversation about your hay deliveries and spreading good luck?"

"Aye, I do." Rhun scratched his head. "But I didn't stop before ye on any of my trips."

"You did better than that. You provided me with a wonderful story to tell a friend who needed a bit of cheering." He held up his pint. "*Lechyd Da.*"

"She must be a beauty if ye're using our old ways to court her." Rhun held up his own glass, cutting off Conway's response. "And the best of health to ye also, Lord Griffith."

Later that night, he leaned back against his pillows and reread her latest letter. With each response, Conway could see her letting down a little more of the wall around her heart. He could also see the progress of her recovery through her words. Lady Helen had gone from proper to friendly to warmly affectionate.

Dear Lord Gwuff,

I do apologize, but rarely is any other name used for you in our household. I fear you will never be called by your proper title when you visit next. Maeve stands next to me as I write this, demanding I send hugs through the envelope. She knows what her name looks like, so she is now smiling, certain her message has been passed along.

The estate is busy preparing for the harvest season. I forgot how much I missed this time of year. We usually have a celebration for the tenants and neighbors after the crops are in. Do you practice the old Celtic traditions at your estate? Maeve assures me you will send some fascinating activities that she must recreate here at Stanfeld Manor. As you write your response, keep in mind that anything you mention will be brought to Gideon. I do believe he may have been cursing you under his breath over the last Lord Gwuff episode. He had to go on quite the scavenger hunt to find seaweed. I never knew the plant could be so entertaining.

Oh, if you could have seen the look on Cook's face when Maeve entered the kitchen with a bucket of it and proudly handed it to her.

"I'll not have that green slime in my kitchen, Miss Maeve. Now off with you," she'd told my little girl with a wag of her finger.

"Well, if you don't mind evil spirits looking over your shoulder while you cook..."

Maeve shook her head with absolute certainty in her eyes, and I swear poor Cook turned pale.

"What does someone as young as you know of evil spirits?" she'd asked cautiously.

"A great lord told me that this"—Maeve shook the bucket at Cook—"will keep them away. What else do we have to know?"

Cook took the bucket—to appease the little one, she said—and promptly tossed it out after Maeve left. But yesterday I went to the kitchen to tell Cook about some unexpected guests. You'll never believe what I saw. In a corner of the room, next to the tinctures she keeps for burns and cuts was a bundle of seaweed hanging from the ceiling, discreetly mixed with the drying mint and lavender.

Your dear friends,

Helen and Maeve

CHAPTER ELEVEN

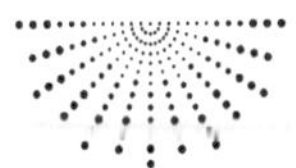

Late October

"All Hallows' Eve is coming, Mama."

Helen looked at her daughter. They were outside, picking the last blades of green grass for Frog. It was one of Maeve's favorite pastimes, and Frog seemed to enjoy it as well. "And what does that mean?"

"Bonfahyuhs and witches. Remembah? I forgot what Lord Gwuff called the day."

She and Griffith, as she thought of him now, continued their correspondence and they grew more companionable with each letter. Maeve now ran to meet the butler when he announced mail, and Sanders always had a happy grin when he was able to hand a letter to his young mistress. She would carefully open the envelope, using her pudgy finger to trace each line looking for her name. She continued to be spellbound by each new tidbit of Welsh folklore he never failed to include for her. After the seaweed debacle, as Gideon now called it, her brother would only hang his head and wait for the next escapade his niece would promise him was most important for both family and staff.

The last letter had Lord Stanfeld sighing with relief when Maeve only asked for a bucket to collect rain. Then she proceeded to collect and wash all the coins the family and staff had in their pockets with the stored water, ensuring it would never be stolen. But the most recent missive had been full of fascinating details about the upcoming and highly celebrated holiday in Wales.

"I may need to take a trip to Wales and have a talk with my good friend," grumbled Gideon good-naturedly. "I'm beginning to think he comes up with some of these to torture me as much as amuse my niece."

But Maeve's sweet smile and earnest requests were never denied. Helen now reread the section of Griffith's letter that spoke of the Celtic holiday.

"Samhain. We never celebrated that. It's more of a pagan ritual." She tousled the girl's hair. "But I imagine we can carve some turnips and put them in the windows."

"I have a pile of wood we can buhn. I collect some evewy day when I walk with Tess." The maid had continued their walks, even with the arrival of Nurse. Mrs. Hampton was a wonderful, nurturing woman, but Tess was much more suited to chasing the child than the older nurse.

"We will talk to your uncle about the kindling. I'm sure he'll manage something that resembles a bonfire."

She thought of Griffith and imagined him before a bonfire, looking wickedly handsome and inviting her to dance. *Stop it!* she scolded herself. The man was creeping into her thoughts too much as of late. He had been invading her dreams too.

"Mama, why are all you clothes black?" She fingered the lace overlay on her mother's bombazine skirt.

Helen brushed the hair from Maeve's cheeks. Familiar blue eyes blinked up at her, curiosity shining in them. "Remember when we talked about your papa going away to Heaven?"

She nodded, her expression serious now.

"Wearing this somber color shows I am sad that he is gone."

Maeve thought about this for a bit, digging her toe in the grass at her feet. "We didn't put on black when Lord Gwuff went away. We love him too."

Her heart clenched at the words of endearment spoken so easily. She crouched down and hugged the little girl close, suddenly feeling quite weepy. Helen shook her head. "That's because he can come back to us. Your papa cannot. But we will go to see him someday."

"When is that?"

"When our time here on earth is done. A long, long time from now."

"Will Papa be lonely?" she asked, her breath tickling Helen's ear.

"No, my sweet. He's with other people who have gone to Heaven too."

"Good. I don't want him to be by himself." And with that, she untangled herself from her mother's embrace and ran toward the stable and Frog. "Will we see Lord Gwuff again? I miss his hugs and when he swings me in the air awound and awound. Don't you want to see him again too?"

"I do," Helen answered. And her breath caught at the realization that she meant it.

. . .

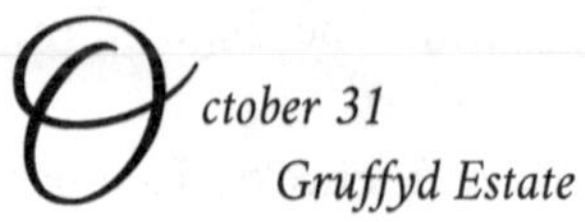

October 31
Gruffyd Estate

The bonfire crackled and spit exploding embers against the midnight sky. There were villagers with masks dancing lively jigs around the growing flames. The faces of the villagers were tinged pink with excitement and alcohol. It was a night of otherworldly happenings. When there was but a thin veil between their world and beyond. A time when loved ones could reach out for a final word. Or enchantments could be cast by evil spirits. It was one of Conway's favorite nights of the year.

Earlier, the cattle had been brought down by the drovers to graze in the summer pastures, and the celebration had begun. As was his family's tradition, the earl provided meat sizzling on spits, wine, ale, cider, and good Scotch whiskey for toasts all around. The tenants had filled two long trestle tables with various dishes and desserts. It was a beautiful, clear evening with a chill in the air but not cold.

"Lord Griffith, I'm here to tell ye that this is the best Samhain yet," said Owen, his new official estate manager. Powys had finally trained the younger man to his own satisfaction and handed over the responsibility. That had been a bittersweet day, and Conway had insisted on retaining the faithful employee in an advisory capacity in addition to his pension.

"It's been an excellent year. I believe in sharing my good fortune." He watched his tenants laugh and dance around the fire. "I couldn't do this by myself." And then a pretty village girl grabbed his hand and pulled him into the dancing circle.

Later, he sat on a stump near the fire, Powys next to him.

"Ye seem to have much on your mind, my lord. It cannot be the estate, for it's prospering, to be sure."

"Aye," agreed Conway, "I'm counting my blessings."

"Then what has ye ruminating with such a serious countenance?" Powys leaned over and poured a bit of whisky from his flask into Conway's cup. "If it's not business, and the countess is well, it must be a woman."

Conway snorted. "Aye, it's a female. You're an astute man."

"That's why ye pay me to advise," Powys said with a chortle. "Tell me about her."

And to Conway's surprise, he did. He began with Bristol and ended with the last letter he'd sent. Somewhere near the end, they'd finished off Powys's flask and started on Conway's.

"Weel," slurred the older man, "have ye tried asking the hazelnut yet?"

"No"—he belched, then hiccupped—"but if you think it will help, I'm willing to try." Conway vaguely remembered the legend of putting a question to the nut to see if one's sweetheart felt the same. When tossed into the fire, the answer was revealed by the way the hazelnut burned and sizzled in the flames.

"I'd think ye have better luck asking yer da—the late Earl of Brecken—for help. If there's ever a night to get an answer, it would be this one."

On his way home, Conway looked up at the bright stars. His eye caught one that seemed to blink bright, then dull, beckoning to him in a code. "Father, if that's you, send me a sign. Do I go after her? Do I continue as I am? God's blood, I love her to distraction."

He looked up as he talked as if the star would reply. Then his face collided with a tree trunk, and he found himself on his arse. Laughter bubbled up his throat and turned into long, loud guffaws. He hiccupped again, then looked back up at the star.

"Well, you either told me to watch where I'm bloody going, or you're trying to knock some sense into me." He rubbed the growing bump on his forehead. "I'll figure out which tomorrow."

CHAPTER TWELVE

December 1820
Gruffyd Estate, Wale

"I've received a letter from Brecken," Conway informed his grandmother at breakfast. He had learned upon his return from London that he would be an uncle. "He'll be taking Evie to London at the end of January. He wants an *accoucheur* to tend to her rather than a midwife."

"Both would be a wise idea. The male doctor may have more book knowledge, but there is nothing to compare with a midwife's experience." Lady Griffith held out her hand for the letter so she could read it herself. She refused to admit it was hard to decipher the script these days. Instead, she had Conway read it aloud, and then she perused the contents as if making sure her grandson had told her correctly.

"He's invited me to join them after the birth. Perhaps stay for part of the Season and meet some young ladies." He took a sip of the bitter coffee and smacked his lips. "What say you?"

"Any particular woman in mind?" she asked nonchalantly.

"No."

"Aren't you still writing to the widow?" Her gaze was fastened on him now.

"Yes. And her name is Mrs. O'Neill, or Lady Helen."

"I thought she'd responded. Regularly. And yes, I would expect her to use her brother's title again and resume her old address in her social circles. Did you hear back from Stanfeld yet?"

He had written to Gideon, mentioning he may be in England on business and hinting at a visit. Gideon had responded he was always welcome. But he would not mention anything to his sister or niece until they set a date, not wanting to disappoint Maeve. But now, with the invitation from Brecken, he had the perfect excuse to meet up with them. Gideon would be in London to take his seat in the Lords. Lady Helen would most likely accompany the family since her sister lived in Town. However, he had one more obstacle here at home before he moved forward with his courtship.

The countess's fork began tapping against the side of the china as his silence lengthened. "What has you so tightlipped this morning?"

He sighed. "Grandmama, you say you want me to take a wife. Yet, I know what Mama went through when she lived here. I'm not sure I want to bring a young woman into that kind of conflict."

"Why—"

"I don't want to hear the excuses. I've heard them all from

both sides." He ran his fingers through his hair and stood, walking over to the sideboard to fill his plate with eggs and rasher. He needed to choose his words carefully.

"Whoever I bring home as my wife, she will need to be in charge of this household." He sat down and reached for a piece of toast from the rack. Finally, he raised his head and matched her glare with his own steady one. "Do you understand what I'm saying?"

"You don't think I can get along with another female under my ro—under *this* roof?" Her lips clamped tightly together, deepening the creases around her mouth. Her dark eyes sparked. "I take umbrage to that."

"Of course you do. But the fact still remains that I cannot marry until this issue is settled." He buttered his toast, waiting for her response.

"I'm sure the girl will need some supervision and training at first. Every household is different," she replied, her chin jutting out. "It was different with your father. He was twice your mother's age."

"You will be looking over her shoulder, making her second guess every move she makes."

"Well, I—"

"Should move into the dowager house." There, he'd said it. But the look of pain that crashed across her face made him regret blurting it out. "Not right away."

"Before the bride crosses the threshold." She took a drink of her chocolate, set it down very precisely, and dabbed the corners of her mouth with a napkin. "You are right, of course. I will begin renovations this week. The décor is deplorable, just deplorable. But we'll right that soon enough. Could you pass me the marmalade?"

And the conversation moved on. Just like that. Conway made a conscious effort to keep his jaw from dropping. He had dreaded this conversation, knew it had to happen, and had procrastinated long enough. He shook his head, then chuckled. His grandmother was an enigma to be sure.

"Now, what's this pishposh about not having a particular lady in mind?" she asked, adding a dollop of orange sweetness to her toast. "You're not one to change his mind."

"No, but I cannot assume Lady Helen feels the same way." He grinned at her raised eyebrow. "Of course, I plan to see her when I go. I've already written Stanfeld again, and we're meeting in London in February. If his sister does not accompany the family, I'll contrive an invitation to his estate."

"That's my boy." Lady Griffith nodded and lifted her spoon. "Show her the Welsh fortitude. And remember to bring some leeks."

Conway threw his head back and laughed. An old superstition that keeping leeks on one during a fight will bring victory. "Love is not a boxing match, Grandmama."

"Oh, how little you know," she murmured, taking a bite of her bread. "Love is always an uphill battle."

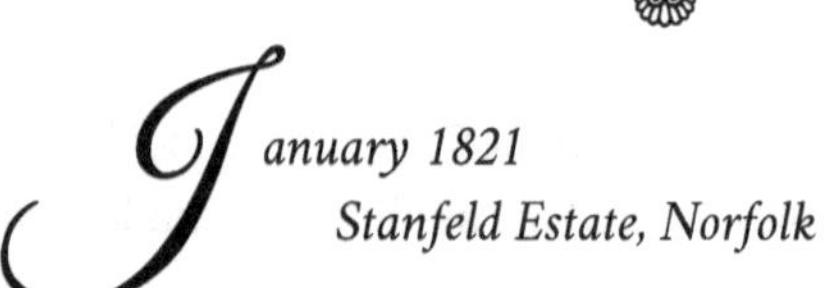

January 1821

Stanfeld Estate, Norfolk

Twelfth Night was over, and Maeve lay in her bed, softly snoring. It had taken a month, but she finally slept in the nursery all night. No more cold little toes sneaking under her counterpane early in the morning. It was bittersweet. And lonely.

She walked into her mother's parlor and plopped onto a chair by the fire. "Off to slumberland."

"She certainly enjoyed the holiday." Her mother looked up, a smile in her deep blue eyes. "And you?"

Helen nodded. "I did, truly. I've been looking forward to the New Year." She tucked one foot beneath her, the other hanging down while her toe tapped the wool carpet. "I think I shall begin wearing some half-mourning colors."

"Oh? Does this have anything to do with a certain letter Gideon received?"

She blushed. "Of course not. Though I consider him a close friend, and it would be nice to see him again."

"Close now, is it? Little Maeve certainly hasn't forgotten the earl. She adored the stuffed Little Bit he sent as a Christmas and birthday gift. She says Aurora now has her own dog." Her mother set down her needlework. "And do not worry that she refuses another doll. I remember a torn and filthy blanket I would not relinquish until I was ten. Your grandmother hated that old rag."

"I assumed Maeve's obsession with the thing was because her father had given it to her."

"That might be part of it. But when we have something that makes us feel happy or safe—or both—we tend not to care what it looks like. It's the feeling it gives us, that security of something that's always been there for us and always will."

Helen nodded. "I hadn't thought of it that way. I suppose you are right. She can choose her own toys."

"Back to Lord Griffith. You've been exchanging letters quite regularly. Any exciting news from Wales?" she asked, one auburn brow arched.

She nodded. "Yes, I mean, no. Yes, we have become… close through our correspondence. He is quite eloquent in his writing. And he makes me laugh at least once with every letter. He is the reason Maeve learned to recognize her name so early."

"Such an accomplished man, our Lord Griffith. And what type of answers do you send in reply?" Her mother bent her head over the needlework again, rocking gently as she worked. "Encouraging?"

"I-I'm not sure how he would interpret my words. I recount on-dits from London that Gideon or Etta have relayed to us, Maeve's reaction to his latest letter, and whatever tidbits I can think of." She picked at her skirt. "I want to see him again, yet the idea frightens me."

"Meeting with a *friend* frightens you?"

"Mama, we both know he seeks more."

"And why is that such a terrible thing?"

She sighed, trying to make sense of her jumbled thoughts. "Love is painful."

"So is not loving."

Helen thought about this. "When I met Rory, he was a whirlwind and knocked me off-balance. I never knew what to think. I just soaked up his excitement, his passion, and followed him." She stood and began pacing. "The gale was wonderful and terrifying, and then… I was left alone and cold. My life went from an adventure to silent and lonely. If it weren't for my daughter, I'm not sure what I might have done. My heart was broken in so many pieces that I don't know if I've put them all back together again."

"Does it feel cracked when you read the earl's letters?"

Helen shook her head. "It feels right, but I was so wrong before. I don't think I could weather that storm again."

Her mother came to her then, put an arm around her shoulder, and pulled her close. "Just listen to your heart, my sweet, and keep your mind open. My heart has never led me wrong."

"But what about—"

"Sometimes we must experience a misdirected or mistaken tenderness to appreciate true love when it finds us.

For it finds *us,* my darling girl, and don't ever think otherwise. I'm not saying that Lord Griffith is the right one, but he may be. And perhaps what you have been through is leading you to the life you are meant for. How will you know if you don't give your heart a chance to speak?"

CHAPTER THIRTEEN

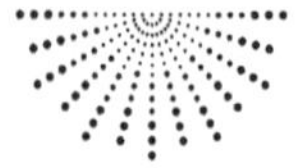

March 1821
A London dinner party

Conway tossed back the brandy. He'd suffered through a ball, a musicale, and Almack's already. He was ogled and looked over like his cattle at auction. And the whispers...

Good stock, one matron had said.

A little short, another had said doubtfully.

Heard he's quite plump in the pocket.

His favorite so far, *But he's Welsh, you know.*

If he wasn't meeting up with Stanfeld tonight, he'd be tempted to send them all to the devil and go home. To Wales. *Because he was Welsh, you know*. He sat in the private billiards room at the Wicked Earls' Club, putting off the inevitable. The sound of ivory clacking against ivory took him from his brooding.

A man in livery appeared at the door. "Your carriage is ready, my lord."

He nodded and rose. "Thank you, I'll be right down." Then he poured another finger of brandy and threw it back. *Now I'm ready.*

The streetlamps glowed a pale yellow over the wet cobblestones. His driver pulled up in front of the large townhouse where he'd once shared a meal with Lady Helen. Tonight, his host would be Lord Stanfeld and his wife. He hadn't met her yet and wondered if Lady Stanfeld knew of him only through her husband or if someone else had mentioned him. He saw a line of several more carriages in front of his own and another pulling up as he reached the portico.

A small dinner party, Stanfeld had said. He had seen his old friend at White's last week. Conway had thought his inquiry of Lady Helen had sounded solicitous without being overly so. He had learned she was in half mourning now and might visit London for some minor social events. The words had stiffened his resolve to remain in Town. Tonight, though, he'd hint at an invitation to Stanfeld's country home.

He handed his hat and overcoat to one of the footmen and proceeded into the crowded drawing room. Conway froze. Lady Helen was sitting in a corner with her sister, Etta, a lovely woman with dark chestnut hair and light brown eyes. Her husband, Lord Burnham, stood behind both women, his hand on his wife's shoulder.

Lady Helen looked up suddenly and blinked, peered around the room, and stopped her gaze on him. Her sapphire eyes grew wide, and a smile curved her plump lips. Conway couldn't move, couldn't look away, couldn't even open his mouth. It had been months since he'd seen her, months since he'd breathed her scent of vanilla and jasmine.

A hand clasped his shoulder. "Good of you to come." Stanfeld stood next to him. "I'd like you to meet my wife."

Conway turned to the lovely woman with burnt umber waves and honey-brown eyes. "Lady Stanfeld, it is wonderful to finally meet you. His description hardly does you justice."

"Why thank you, Lord Griffith. It's a pleasure to meet ye. It seems ye have an avid admirer in our house." He had expected her warm smile, but the thick brogue surprised him.

His heart sped up. Had Lady Helen spoken of him? "I'm pleased to hear it." Did he sound mundane or mildly interested? He was hoping for mildly interested.

"My niece, Maeve, believes the sun rises and sets on the wisdom of the great Welshman, Lord Gwuff." Stanfeld laughed and clapped Conway on the shoulder again. "You made quite the impression on the girl."

But what about the other girl? he wanted to ask.

"Tell me of your new nephew, Griffith. I hear Brecken is ecstatic to have his heir."

Conway told them of the birth of a boy. "He looks like his father but has the hair and eyes of his mother. And a healthy set of lungs on him."

"Was it a difficult birth?" asked Lissie.

"According to the women, it was not."

"I'm happy for her. Lady Brecken is a lovely woman."

"You know her?" Did everyone in England know each other, Conway wondered.

"Her sister Fenella married Gideon's cousin, Lachlan MacNaughton."

"Ah, a small world, indeed."

"Have you spoken with my sister yet?" asked Stanfeld.

Conway shook his head. "I've only just arrived. I was hoping to—"

And then she was there, her fiery red curls caught up in a ribbon and cascading down her neck, pearls dangling at her ears and around her throat. She wore a silk dress of mauve with a matching satin overlay. Black lace trim offset the edges of the cuffs and hem. *Perfection.* He drank in the sight of her, intoxicated by her nearness and the scent of jasmine with a hint of vanilla.

"Lord Griffith," she said, "it's been much too long." She held out a gloved hand.

The woman he'd escorted from Bristol was gone. In her place stood a lady at home in this social setting. She had put on some weight, and the gaunt look was gone. Creamy skin and rosy cheeks were only enhanced by her smile.

He took her fingers in his and kissed the back of her glove. "Lady Helen, it is my pleasure. I am happy to see you fully recovered."

"No doubt, thanks to you," Stanfeld said. "I heard all about the harrowing escapade of my niece, and your ensuing rescue of both damsels in distress at the docks."

"The girl has a vivid imagination, so I'm sure the whole incident has been somewhat embellished." He could feel his cheeks burning. "It wasn't nearly so dramatic."

"I beg to disagree," cut in Lady Helen. "She dashed in front of the carriage, and Lord Griffith dove onto the ground, scooped her up, and rolled away from the moving wheels."

"We owe ye a debt of gratitude, my lord," said Lady Stanfeld.

Lady Helen placed her hand on his arm, and heat shot through his body. "I was so shocked by how close she'd come to harm, I fainted. Then he had to carry me."

"I'd do it again," he murmured, scanning her face. This time, she blushed.

Conway accepted a glass of wine, and Stanfeld introduced him to some of the other guests. "Can I ask you a question?" asked his host as they paused in a corner, away from other ears.

"Anything."

"What is going on between you and my sister? And do not tell me you are only friends who enjoy corresponding with one another." Stanfeld's dark eyes pinned him, waiting for an answer.

Conway looked around, then over his shoulder. No one was close enough to hear his response, and Lady Helen stood across the room with her sister-in-law. "Are you sure you want to know?"

His friend nodded, eyes narrowing.

"I'm in love with her."

He was silent for a moment, then a wide grin covered his face. "Excellent, Griff. I'm happy to hear it."

"And Lady Helen? Do you know if she holds any affection for me?" Did his voice go up as he asked? *Good God.*

Stanfeld bent closer. "The feeling is mutual, according to my mother. It's just convincing her marriage is worth another try. But I have a feeling if anyone can do it, it's a stubborn Welshman."

Conway laughed. She cared for him. His heart soared, and he wanted to shout it to the room. "I only needed to know this wasn't one-sided. I'm in no hurry. I'm already thirty-two blasted years old. What's a bit longer?"

"That's the spirit," agreed Stanfeld. "And know that you have her family behind you. Now, what can we do to help?"

"First, tell me whose idea it was for her to come to Town."

"Hers. Lissie mentioned being nervous about hosting her first London dinner party, and Helen offered to assist." He nodded toward the women. "They have become close these past months."

"Your sister knew I would be here?" He held his breath.

"Yes. She did hesitate for a moment when I informed her, then shrugged, and said she must pack and make arrangements for little Maeve." He rubbed his palms together. "Now, how can we be of assistance?"

Conway let out the breath. "Do you plan to stay here long?"

"No, Lissie prefers the country as does Helen. I'll travel back and forth as needed to take my seat at the Lords. Would you like an invitation?"

"You have no idea how happy that would make me." He chanced a glance at the most beautiful woman in the room. "I wouldn't happen to be sitting next to her at dinner, would I?"

Stanfeld snorted. "What do you think?"

"My appetite just grew tenfold." He tipped his wine toward Stanfeld and turned to the prize. For at this moment, he had no doubt he would win her heart. Thinking of a curly-haired girl with eyes like her mother, he thought, *I'm already halfway there.*

Helen felt his eyes on her. Looking over her shoulder, she caught Griffith staring at her as he listened to something Gideon said. Were they conspiring? *Don't be a ninny.* Her brother didn't know her feelings—she barely knew her own feelings. But tonight, when Griffith walked into the room, she'd felt the air sizzle. Her pulse had raced; her stomach flipped. She hadn't realized how strongly he affected her until she'd seen him again.

Now he was walking toward her, looking so handsome with his dark hair smoothed back, the snug waistcoat and tails, that smile… Then the happiness knotted with anxiety as she remembered the same excitement with Rory.

They are different men.

His breath was warm when he leaned down close and whispered, "May I escort you to the dining room?"

Helen pushed Rory from her mind. "That would be lovely."

Dinner was announced, and the entire group moved toward the door. They were seated next to each other. Trying to tamp down the fluttering wings, she put her hand on her belly. *How will I manage to eat a bite?*

Yet, she did. Griffith kept filling her plate while maintaining the conversation. For a man who claimed to be stilted in social circles, he was very much at ease tonight. Charming, in fact. He told her of his journey to London over soup. Regaled her with his escapades as a child while serving roast mutton and vegetables. Through the salads and cheeses and another main course, he told an amusing account of his half brother's experience as a new father. By the time the nuts, fruits, and sweetmeats were served, Helen could only nibble on a hazelnut.

The ladies retired to the drawing room, leaving the men to their port.

"Dinner seemed to go well," Lissie said as the ladies found seats. "Yer Welshman is verra handsome."

"He's not *my* Welshman, but I do agree with you. On both points." Her sister-in-law had become a close confidante, another sibling. "I don't know if I'm ready."

"Then take yer time. I dinna think he'll mind waiting." Lissie hooked arms with Helen, and they walked the room to socialize with the other guests. Some had brought their needlework; others simply enjoyed sharing gossip.

An hour later, the men joined them, and tea was served. Four guests began a game of whist. A viscount had brought his violin and accompanied his wife on the pianoforte while their daughter sang. Everyone clapped, and someone suggested charades. Helen was about to join the game when Griffith appeared at her side.

"Would you like to stroll in the garden?" he asked. "It's a bit chilly but a clear night."

"It's a small one, but a walk after that meal would be nice. I'll get my cloak." She had decided there were some advantages to her situation. No one would gasp at a widow taking a short stroll outside with a gentleman. She returned with her cloak, informed Lissie of where she was going, and took Griffith's offered arm.

They walked in companionable silence during the first turn around the garden. Griffith pointed out several constellations. "Do you see the bright star just to our left? Can you see Taurus?"

"No, I'm afraid I don't know the night sky very well," she said, peering up at the thousands of diamonds sparkling above.

"Here," he said, bending his knees so he stood in front of her but lower than her line of sight. "Follow my finger and I'll trace it. It's supposed to be a bull, though without a telescope it's hard to distinguish."

Helen leaned forward, using his finger as a center. He described the legs and horns, but she could not see the form of an animal. "I'm sorry. I do see the outline you are showing me, but for the life of me, I can't see a bull."

Rising, Griffith turned to face her, and his head collided with hers. She yelped and covered her nose, the sharp pain bringing tears to her eyes.

"Blast it! I'm sorry." He stepped closer and covered her hand with his. "Let me see it."

His fingers gently pressed around her nose. His image before her was blurry, so she blinked rapidly to bring him into focus. As he became clear, his dark chocolate eyes connected with hers. "I don't think it's broken."

Helen could feel his breath against her skin. If she tilted her head forward just a degree, they would touch. He smelled of bergamot and night air, and his lips were right there, so close, so soft… She reached up with her gloved hand and brushed his mouth, then pulled it back, realizing what she had done. *Sweet Mary, why did I do that?* Her gaze traveled back to his, and she could see the hunger now.

"I promised myself I wouldn't do this, but…" Griffith cupped her cheek with his hand and touched his lips to hers.

A sweet brush, a hint of port. Then he pulled her close and kissed her hungrily. He smelled so good; his body was hard and pressing. A warmth spread from her belly, lower, and that familiar tumbling in her stomach came rushing back.

His tongue traced the seam of her lips, and she opened for him. His thumb stroked her cheek, his other palm remained steady and caressing on her back. Her head swam, her body thrummed, and she gave in to her desires. Her arms went around his neck, and she almost smiled against his mouth when he groaned.

Eyes closed, she reveled in the velvet of his tongue against hers, remembering her innate passion, simmering below the surface. She remained still when he ended the kiss, breathing heavily, trying to still the squall within her. Finally, Helen opened her eyes. And the emotion in his was her undoing.

She pushed away from him, shaking her head. "I shouldn't have… We can't…"

"Lady Helen, stop." His voice, deep and hoarse, stilled her, but she did not turn around. She felt his breath stirring her hair as he came up behind her. "You understand why I'm in London, yes?"

She nodded, not trusting her voice.

"I'm hoping to find a wife." His fingers curled around her arm and slowly spun her until she faced him. He tipped her chin up. "Look at me."

Helen slowly raised her eyes and swallowed. "You mentioned it in your last letter."

"And you must know how much I've come to care for you," he whispered in her ear, stroking her cheek with his knuckles. "I'd like to ask you—"

"Don't say it, please. Don't ask me to marry you." She cursed the tear that rolled down her face. "I cannot think of marriage now."

"It's bad manners to interrupt, you know." He cupped her face with both hands, kissed her eyes closed, her nose, and finally her mouth. An easy, lazy kiss that promised so much. "I would like to return to Stanfeld when you go. Your brother invited me. I thought we could spend time together. Get to know each other through spoken words rather than only letters. You are still in mourning, my lady. I will give you the time you need. Will you at least allow me your company for a week or two?"

Helen placed her gloved hands over his and looked at him, her lip trembling. But she nodded.

"Good. I'd like to see Lake Perfect." He leaned his forehead against hers. "I promise not to ask for more than you are willing to give."

"And if I'm not willing to marry again?" she asked, wondering how she could deny this man anything.

"I would never jeopardize our friendship. It is too dear to me." His fingers pulled on the strings of her cloak, and he retied them for her. Then he threaded her hand through his arm and kissed her cheek. "I will warn you, however, that I'm a Welshman. We're known to be slow and steady—and stubborn. Patience is one of my virtues."

CHAPTER FOURTEEN

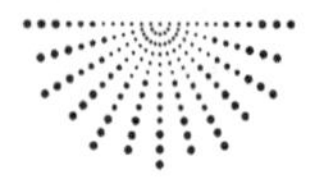

A week later
Stanfeld Estate

Spring came early to Norfolk. Helen had hoped to go ice skating with Griffith and Maeve when he arrived. Tomorrow. *He will be here tomorrow.*

What had she been thinking to agree to this? A widow. In mourning. Well, half mourning. Still... why wasn't her mother or brother telling her how inappropriate this visit was? Why did Lissie just smile and hum when Helen voiced her concerns? Because Helen was an adult and would have to make her own decisions. Her dreams had not helped. Griffith on a horse, chasing her down while she laughed and lifting her into the saddle with him. Griffith in the stable, brushing his horse, his shirt open, sweat clinging to the muscles of his back. It didn't matter the scenario; they all ended with a kiss. A ravenous, delicious, life-changing kiss.

But she'd had these feelings before and been wrong. How

could she be certain? She had Maeve to think of now. But her daughter adored the man. She had cried a few times once she realized she wouldn't see her father for a very long time. Then Lord Gwuff and his letters had filled a void along with *Uncle Gidjun.* If it was up to her family, she would be wed on the morrow when the earl arrived.

Little Bit nosed her hand. She put down the brush, fed Frog the last carrot, and squatted down to scratch the terrier's wiry coat. "Tell me all will be well, Little Bit." His tail wagged faster. "That's not an answer," she said, then kissed the top of his head and straightened up. It was late, but she couldn't sleep. The horses, their nickers, the soothing sound of munching hay always settled her nerves. *The sun will shine again.* But would it shine this week? Would it shine on Lord Griffith?

Lissie met her at the door of the house. "Restless?" she asked.

"Yes." With a sigh, Helen hugged her sister-in-law. "I'm feeling unsettled."

"I was going to the library to look for a book. Would ye like to join me?"

The women perused the shelves. Lissie pulled out a thick history tome. "This should be dull enough to put ye to sleep."

Helen flipped a few pages of the book. She chewed her bottom lip, then blurted out, "How did you know the love you had for Gideon was different from what you had with your first husband?"

"Ah." She took Helen's hand, and they moved to the wingback chairs by the hearth. "Ian and I were betrothed as children. It was an agreement between clans."

"I didn't know that. He was a MacNaughton, my cousin, but I didn't realize the Scots still did that." What would it be like to marry a man because of an agreement?

"We loved each other, no doubt. But as we've discussed

before, it was a different kind of love. Fierce in its own way, but no' the same as the burning passion I feel now. He was my best friend." Lissie paused, then leaned forward, and took Helen's hand. "The heart kens what we need. I listened to my heart, and it led me to Gideon. If I had fought that urge, I would have been miserable without him."

"But what if my heart doesn't know?" She chewed her lip. "It was so tumultuous, loving Rory. And so short. By the time I was pregnant, that excitement, the fierce desire to be together was already fading. I realized I didn't *like* him, though I loved him. Do you like my brother?"

"Aye, of course. That's the foundation all couples must have to manage the years together. When passions rise and fall, the friendship remains to get us through until the next wave of desire. If ye love someone, truly love someone, it's not heat and hunger every day." Lissie laughed. "It doesna go away, but it burns more brightly at times. Does that make sense?"

Helen nodded.

"Ye have grown to like this mon?"

"Yes, our correspondence has indeed forged a warm friendship. He's a good man."

"And ye've kent him longer than yer first husband when ye eloped?"

Helen looked into Lissie's warm golden eyes and saw the compassion there. "So, I'm halfway there?"

Lissie nodded. "Now ye must let yer heart decide."

Griffith had abandoned the carriage for the last leg of the trip. He needed air and exercise to ward off the nervousness coming over him. His confidence had begun to wane in the last ten miles, and enjoying the countryside from a saddle always restored his good humor. Stanfeld Manor came into view, its fairytale turrets shining in the afternoon sun. It was a grand estate, but Conway preferred the wilder lands of Wales. So much of England was too orchestrated, plotted out, with nature bent to the will of man instead the other way around.

Trotting through the gate, he heard the familiar bark of Little Bit. He guessed Maeve would be close behind. And he was right. The brown and white little mutt came barreling around the house from the stables, a little dark-haired girl running behind. She was waving at him and yelling something, but Conway wasn't sure if it was directed at him or the dog.

"Lord Gwuff, I missed you," she shouted.

He pulled his horse to a stop and dismounted. His feet had barely hit the ground when a little body came flying at him. He bent and scooped her up, her pudgy arms going around his neck. Any misgivings he'd had dissolved with that sweet, tight hug. He thought his heart would burst when she planted a loud kiss on his cheek. This was right; this was where he should be.

"I've missed you too, my little princess." He bent down to pet Little Bit with Maeve still clinging tightly to his neck and giggling.

"I like it when you call me that." She smooshed her cheek against his and whispered in his ear, "Guess what?"

"What?"

"I'm foaherrrrr now," she announced proudly, holding up four fingers.

"Oh my, all grown up." He set her down on her own feet, noting the effort she used on her pronunciation. "And when did this magnanimous event occur?"

"In Decembah. Errr."

"Did you get my present?"

She nodded. "Mama says he's the only dog who can sleep with me."

A stable boy stood patiently, waiting to take Conway's horse. The carriage was just coming over the hill toward the gate. The great double doors of the manor opened, and Sanders appeared. He was followed by Stanfeld and his wife. And Lady Helen.

Breathe, you lodcock! Say something. He didn't try to wipe the crooked grin from his face. Instead, he stepped forward to shake Gideon's hand.

"Griffith, I hope the journey was pleasant?" asked Stanfeld, holding out his hand and clapping Conway on the shoulder.

Lady Helen wore a soft gray dress with lavender trim. It clung to her curves as she walked down the steps, and she nervously smoothed her ruby curls into place. He saw the uncertainty in her blue eyes and longed to hold her again. Tell her how bright their future was, to let him love her, love Maeve, and give her the family they both so desperately wanted.

"Aye, the weather held," he said, not taking his eyes from Lady Helen. "You look lovely."

"Thank you," she said, her cheeks pink. "I see my daughter is already monopolizing your time."

"One of my favorite females," he agreed as Maeve slid her tiny hand into his big one.

"Well, come in. Mrs. Laskey is arranging for tea in the drawing room." Lady Stanfeld led the way into the house.

The dowager countess joined them for tea. "It's so good to see you again, Lord Griffith," she said, offering her hand. "My granddaughter has quite a schedule of events planned for the week."

"I'm ready for anything," he exclaimed, giving a side-glance to Lady Helen.

❦

It had taken three dinners and three attempts to finally have Lady Helen alone in the garden with him. It was a beautiful, chilly night. The sky twinkled with light, and their breath created clouds that seemed to float up to meet the stars. But nothing shone as brightly as the woman beside him. "The sole was quite good at dinner. I noticed you still enjoy custard."

She laughed. "I do forget my manners when it comes to that dessert. I'm afraid I scrape the plate clean."

"It's the small joys in life that often bring us the most pleasure." He curled his fingers into his palms as a stray curl floated against her porcelain cheek. How he craved to tuck it behind her ear, sweep her into his arms…

"What is your favorite sweet, Griffith?"

"Apple tarts. Nothing better in this world than a fresh apple tart drizzled with honey." He winked at her. "Except, perhaps, a kiss from you."

She stopped and looked up at him, then the mirth shone in her blue eyes. "You're flirting with me!"

"Lady Helen, I would never stoop to such trickery for your affections." He put his hand over his heart, knowing his smirk gave him away.

"Do you have a favorite color?"

"Blue."

She arched a brow. "Light blue or dark blue?"

He bit the inside of his cheek to maintain a straight face. "MacNaughton blue."

"You *are* flirting with me," she giggled and slapped his arm.

"I admit to it only if it's working," he acknowledged with a bow, taking her arm and continuing their stroll.

"I do believe there's a bit of a rake hiding inside the introvert."

"You seem to bring out the best in me." Conway marveled at the difference between the reticent widow he had collected on the docks of Bristol and this witty, engaging woman who now walked on his arm.

"Lady Helen, I..." He stopped and turned to face her. "I believe you know my feelings toward you."

She shook her head. "I'm not ready—"

"For such serious conversations? I understand. I am here so we may become better acquainted and more comfortable with each other. Your correspondence has been wonderful and amusing. But I cannot read the expression on your face, the downturn of those lovely lips, the questions in your eyes." He placed his palm on her cheek, struggling to find the right words. "I'm a patient and, I hope, an understanding man. I feel as if I've waited for you all my life. I'm in no hurry now that I've found you."

With a pounding heart, he leaned down and brushed her lips. The heat rushed through his body as if a floodgate had opened. *Good God,* how he needed this woman. His heart, his body, his mind screamed that she was the woman fate had meant for him. Could he convince her in the two weeks they had together?

Conway's free hand went to her waist, feeling her warmth even through her spencer. Her body trembled. With need? As his did? He pulled her against him, letting her feel his passion.

Her gaze locked with his, desire flaring in those cerulean depths. *You may not admit it yet, my love, but you want me as badly as I want you,* he thought as his control wavered.

He claimed her mouth with all the urgency that had built up over the last months. Her closeness, the scent of jasmine and vanilla, her softened curves that fit perfectly against him combined into the perfect storm. When he moaned softly against her lips, her hands went around his neck. Pulling her close, breaths mingling, he closed his eyes and let his fantasies become reality. His tongue caressed the seam of her mouth, and she opened for him, tasting of custard and honey. Their tongues met, and he thought he would die of the pleasure. When her fingers stroked the back of his neck and tugged on strands of his hair, his restraint was tested.

Reluctantly, he pulled back, his knuckles trailing down her cheek. His thumb seemed to move over her bottom lip of its own accord. Her chest heaved, dragging in deep breaths. Her lips were swollen from their kiss. Her eyes told him what he knew already. Oh, how he wanted to speak words of love to her. But the voice of reason told him to move slowly.

"Lady Helen, I will not do this again until you are of the same mind. I will let you initiate our next... intimate moment. But I wanted to make sure you understood how I feel. So until the next time"—he kissed the top of her head, chuckled at the glazed blue of her eyes, and slid her hand around his elbow again—"we shall work at becoming the very best of friends."

CHAPTER FIFTEEN

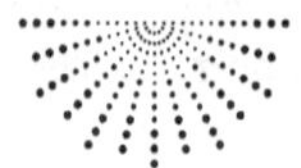

By the second week, Helen almost felt sorry for Griffith. *Almost.* Then she thought of the poor gardener who had to pick leeks and attach them to the roof to ward off sickness for the family and staff.

"He certainly has fortitude," exclaimed her mother as they watched the earl and an enthusiastic if awkward young girl play shuttlecock. "Have you been enjoying yourself?"

Helen sighed. "Very much." Most of the activities during the day included little Maeve. But the evenings were for the adults and included music, games, and walks in the garden. She had seen the shy side of Griffith during a dinner party with the neighboring estate owners. An urge to protect him had come over her, and Helen had intervened during any awkward conversations. His look of gratitude had warmed her and made her feel… needed. Wanted. Not for her family's wealth or position, but for her support, her presence.

"Tomorrow you are going on a picnic?"

"Yes. I'm taking him to Lake Perfect," said Helen. "Cook is preparing a basket."

"I was wondering if you might leave little Maeve here

with me." Her mother kept her eyes on the shuttlecock match. "Lady Carrington is coming for tea and bringing her granddaughter. I believe she's eight or nine. I think Maeve will be a nice distraction for the girl while us old women chat. Then you can skip the carriage and ride. We've a new pony you might like to try."

She studied her mother's profile, suspicious of the nonchalant tone. "Maeve prefers to ride with Griffith. And wouldn't that be improper? For just the two of us, alone, on a picnic?"

"*Pfft.* You're a widow, not some virginal debutante. Besides, who's to know except family?" She turned and patted Helen's cheek. "You need time alone with the man, my dear."

It was true. Griffith—Conway, he was insisting she call him now—had not attempted to kiss her again since the night in the garden. She wasn't sure how she felt about that. He had promised he would let her set the pace, but he was a man after all. In his defense, there was always someone nearby. Added to that were the vile seeds of doubt, nurtured by her insecurity. Rory had been affectionate and passionate, and she'd mistaken it for love. He'd parroted her own words to mollify his token English bride. Was Conway just looking for a wife? Yes, he cared for her. But the word "love" had never been mentioned. Did he love her? And would that be better, or worse, if he did?

After his kiss, her mind had been in turmoil and her heart in pandemonium. She wanted him, but she was afraid to want him. Another kiss might help. Or turn her brain to mush. Her fingers went to her lips as she watched Conway reach out to hit the feather game piece and send it back to his exuberant opponent. He wore a cream shirt, matching trousers, and a light-blue waistcoat. Muscles stretched the thin linen of his shirt as he dove for the return. When he missed, hitting the ground, he looked over at the ladies with the sweetest, silliest grin on his face. Her stomach tumbled. *Admit it. You're falling in love with him.*

As if reading her thoughts, her mother said, "Yes, some time alone would be good for both of you."

❦

Helen ambled through the garden on her way to meet Griffith at the stable. She wore a new riding habit of deep blue merino wool that matched her eyes, a coordinating jacket with Peruvian trimmings about the bust and cuffs. Her half boots and hat were of the same color but a shade lighter, with plumes of feathers dancing above her head. She had seen a picture of it in *La Belle Assemblée* when she was still in Dublin. She had seen a picture of it in *La Belle Assemblée* when she was still in Dublin. Maire's employer had given her an outdated copy and the two had devoured the pages, dreaming of better days. It had been the first piece of clothing she'd ordered herself.

Approaching the stable, she saw Griffith leading out two horses. His own black gelding and a pretty chestnut mare with a blonde mane and tail. Frog had been slightly lame after a hard landing over a hedge, so Helen had decided to try out the new pony.

When Griffith looked her way and smiled, her stomach flipped. Would that ever change? Would he always have this effect on her? She waved back and tucked her riding crop under her arm.

"I see you're alone. Is anything wrong with the little princess?" His grin was contagious, and she returned it, shaking her head.

"No, Mama has a friend visiting with her granddaughter. She thought they might keep each other company. Maeve adores meeting new people." And indeed, her daughter had been very excited to make a new friend. "I'm afraid it's just the two of us for the day."

An entire day.

Alone with this man.

And her dreams and desires.

Sweet Mary, she thought, *this is a terrible idea.*

And then he was next to her, his heat spreading from his hand, through her fingers, and down her belly. Helen couldn't have uttered the word "no" if she'd wanted to.

He helped her up the steps of the riding block and held the rein while she mounted the side saddle. Once her full skirts were settled, hat secured, and the crop in her right hand, a mischievous voice whispered in her head, *Enjoy this time. Enjoy yourself with this handsome man.*

Griffith came up next to her on his taller horse, and they left the yard at a leisurely walk. "Do you ride often, my lord?" she asked, wanting to fill the silence.

"Aye, every day."

"Even in the rain?"

"Even in the rain. I have a stern constitution, so my grandmother tells me."

"Tell me about her." Helen knew he'd been raised half the year by his grandmother and half the year by his mother and stepfather. Gideon had told her Griffith had been the second son, the first son dying in a riding accident at fifteen.

"As you know, I had a brother who had an untimely death. My father had lost his first wife during the birthing. I'm told he truly loved her and took her passing hard. But my grandmother said it was nothing compared to the loss of my brother." He paused, his mouth tightening for a moment. "He finally agreed with Grandmama, agreeing to marry and produce another heir. Unfortunately, they didn't agree on the bride."

"Your grandmother didn't like your mother?"

He shook his head. "That is a very mild way of putting it. My father was more than twice her age. She was beautiful, came from a decent family, but had no wealth to speak of. My grandmother thought he could have done much better, and I believe had someone else picked out."

"More mature?" she asked, wondering if she would like Lady Griffith.

"Aye, and more malleable."

"Your mother was outspoken?"

Griffith snorted. "No, not at all. But she wouldn't be pushed around, either. So, it was a silent battle on her side and a not-so-silent battle on my grandmother's. My mother told my grandmother that she should be living in the dowager house. My grandmother replied she would as soon as she knew her daughter-in-law was *capable*."

Helen gasped. "No!"

"Aye, I'm afraid there was no love lost between them. In her defense, my father had just died, and my mother was with child. It was not an ideal situation for either of them."

"Yet you seem so fond of your grandmother."

He laughed. "She has an icy exterior, but she loves me with all her heart. I believe if my mother had not remarried, they would have found a compromise and became friends. They had me in common."

"Is your grandmother the reason you have waited so long to marry?" Helen wondered if she was being intrusive, but he'd piqued her interest.

"No. She's mellowed with age and wants me to be happy. My wife will provide grandchildren. In fact, she's renovating the dowager house while I'm away. Just in case…" He locked eyes on her. "She's optimistic for this Season and hoping I will come home betrothed."

"And your mother?"

"Ah, my lovely mother. She found love when I was still a babe. My grandmother insisted I live with her, as I was the earl and had responsibilities. My mother, of course, insisted I live with her."

"And your stepfather?"

"Ha! My hero, a wise man who knew the value of compromise." Griffith's eyes glistened, a sad smile curving his mouth. "I miss him still. I never knew my own father, and Brecken was generous with his knowledge and his love."

"He guided you?"

"More than that. He shaped me into the man I've become. He made sure I had a dependable estate manager to teach me about my properties and tenants. I lived with him and my mother from planting season until harvest, learning the land and livestock. I spent the rest of the year at Gruffyd Estate, practicing all the lessons I'd learned."

"And you were close to your half brother?" Helen was intrigued by Griffith's unusual upbringing. An only child half the year, and an older brother and part of a family the other half.

"He's my closest friend. He's family. There's not a man alive I trust more."

"And now you have a nephew."

He grinned. "Who's built like a little Welshman, thick and strong. I think I loved the lad at the first bubble he spit at me."

Helen giggled. "They are messy little beasts, aren't they?"

A breeze kicked up, sending her feathers fluttering above her head. She batted at one while sidestepping a soft spot in the ground made by a tunneling vole.

Griffith studied her hat, opened his mouth, and then shut it again, stirring her curiosity.

"What were you going to say?" she asked.

"It was a question," he said as his cheeks turned red. "But I realized it might be improper."

"I believe we know each other well enough for you to ask. If it's too personal, I shall tell you."

"Your hat… is lovely, of course, but how does it stay on? Those feathers fly this way and that, and you have an abundance of hair. What keeps it from falling off when you trot or canter?"

"That is your scandalous question?" She laughed. "I expected something much more outrageous."

"I never had the nerve to ask a lady. If I asked my grandmother, she would assume I was interested in whatever female was nearby on a horse wearing a hat." He shrugged. "I'm curious how the opposite sex maintains their feminine mystique."

Helen reached up and pulled a long pin from her hat and waved it at him. "No witchery involved, my good sir. Just many, many pins."

He shuddered dramatically. "I'm happy to be a man then. Riding astride and pulling the hat low on my forehead is much safer than sharp objects pointed at my head."

"Well, let's put it to the test, shall we?" With a sly side-glance, Helen kicked the horse with her left foot and slapped its side with her crop, sending the mare into a canter and then a gallop.

"The deuce of a girl," she heard him say behind her as he urged his horse to catch up. They rode across a grazing pasture, scattering a flock of sheep and laughing at the annoyed bleats. They took two hedges, both horses sailing over them easily, and came to a stop before a small copse of trees.

"You're an excellent rider, Lady Helen," Griffith remarked as he caught his breath.

She drew in deep gulps of air, enjoying the exertion. "I

love the speed of a horse and the wind on my face. That magical feeling when my mare is airborne, and we execute the perfect jump."

"You would love Wales, I think. It's as green as England but wilder. The mountains are more rugged, the water bluer, the trees taller. It's a land that gets into your blood, and when you cross the border, you miss it. With all your soul."

"That's high praise from a man of few words." She smiled, enjoying the passion in his eyes. "And the people?"

"Ah, the people are full of superstitions, as you know, but also camaraderie. A neighbor in trouble becomes a problem for the entire village. The Welsh work hard and play hard. There's a celebration for everything, a reward for every hardship endured throughout the year." He grinned. "Of course, I'm a bit prejudiced."

The sun came out from behind a cloud, and Griffith took off his coat. "Excuse the impropriety."

"I wish I could join you," she said, thinking how nice it would be to remove the sturdy spencer.

"You could unbutton your jacket. I won't tell you if you don't." He wiggled his dark brows, making her giggle.

So, she did and felt giddy as he watched her fingers move from her throat to her bodice. Then she forgot about manners, lifted her head to the sun, and enjoyed the cool breeze through the thin muslin of her shirt as they ambled toward the lake. She felt wicked, decadent. Alive. And the day was only beginning.

CHAPTER SIXTEEN

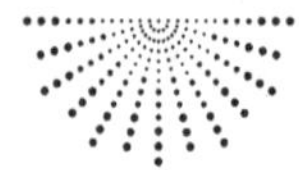

"It's as lovely as its name." Conway dismounted, assisted Helen, then hobbled the horses to let them graze on the fresh spring grass. "Thank you for bringing me here."

Lady Helen spread the blanket on the ground, and Conway set down the basket. Her riding habit showed off her blue eyes, he thought. The form-fitting material showed off her petite but curvy figure. After their gallop, they had both been warm. He had removed his coat, then encouraged her to unbutton her spencer. He had been rewarded with a glimpse beneath, revealing a thin muslin shirt outlining the soft swell of her breasts. A few stray strands of that glorious ruby-red hair lay against her cheek and neck, and he watched her swat them out of the way. She was stunning.

He glanced at the pond, heard the bullfrogs join in the late afternoon birdsong.

"Are they some of your friends?" he asked with a grin.

"Ha! Go ahead and make fun. I'm used to it."

"So that's a *yes*?"

She tossed a napkin at him; he threw it back and

plopped down on the blanket. It was a nice setting, he thought. There were willow trees on each end of Lake Perfect. They were set up next to one, preferring the warm sunshine to the shade. A pair of wrought-iron benches sat side by side on the other end, beneath the second willow. He lay down, pointing up to the big fluffy clouds.

"Looks like sheep," he said.

"I can see that," she agreed, "much easier than the constellation of Taurus you showed me." Then her cheeks went pink as they both remembered what happened that night in the garden.

"Your turn. You find one."

She joined him on the blanket and lay down next to him, her hand over her eyes as she searched the puffs of white. "There, an owl. See its pointed ears and the outline of the wings?"

"Very good. You've played this game before." He rolled to his side, propping himself up with his elbow. "They say when an owl hoots between houses, a maid will lose her chastity." He tried to wipe the sly grin off his face but couldn't. A fierce urge to imitate an owl swept over him.

"Well, it's a good thing there are no owls in the afternoon, and I'm no maid," she quipped back.

He let out a loud guffaw. He picked up her hand and kissed the palm. "Touché! I enjoy a quick wit."

They munched on hard cheese, soft bread, and cold fowl. Cook had also packed some ratafia, which Lady Helen drank from the bottle and handed to Conway. "It's not strong, so enjoy as much as you'd like. I'm sorry we don't have any glasses."

"I'd share all I have with you."

Her eyes locked with his. "I believe you."

"I wanted to thank you for an enjoyable visit so far." He

handed her back the sweet wine mixture as if he hadn't just ripped his chest open and handed her his heart.

"I noticed you were quiet during the dinner party. It was the first time I'd seen you so reserved." She tipped back the bottle and swallowed.

He watched her throat move as the wine flowed. Her neck was long and graceful, and Conway wanted to reach up and stroke it with his fingers, followed by his lips. "The Griffith you know is the same man my family knows, and the villagers I grew up with. With strangers, as I told you, I'm much more reticent."

"Yet, not with me or my family? Why?"

"That's the question I've been asking myself." He reached out and took her hand, his thumb rubbing the back of it. Her skin was like satin.

"And have you found the answer?" Her voice was quiet, barely above a whisper. The wind picked up, ruffling the edges of the blankets, but their gazes remained steady on each other.

"No," he said with a chuckle. "But it *is* how I realized you are the one. You are the woman I've been waiting for, longing for. Loving you filled the hollow place in my heart."

His control crumbled. He sat up, leaned forward, and touched his mouth to hers. Her chest rose up and down with her rapid breathing as he pulled back. "May I kiss you?"

"Wh-what was that?"

"That was just a taste, a prelude. May I kiss you now?" The pounding of his heart surged to his groin, and he thought he would die if she said no. But she nodded shyly.

He leaned forward again, brushing her lips, a whisper of a groan escaping. "I've been thinking of that kiss last week every waking moment. When I close my eyes, I dream of so much more."

His arm snaked around her waist, and he pulled her onto

his lap. The feel of her soft bottom against his manhood was a glorious torture. Slowly, he pulled on the white ribbon, unraveling it until the hat slid off and fell on the blanket. He tucked a red lock behind her ear and stroked her cheek with his knuckles. "You are stunning," he murmured as his lips crashed onto hers, devouring her, demanding she return his passion.

And she did. One hand slid around his neck, her fingers threading through his hair. His mouth traced the curve of her collarbone, trailing up to her jaw, and back to her sweet lips. Something wet plopped on his head. Then another, and another.

"Either a bird is being very naughty, or it's begun to rain," he murmured against her mouth. "Perhaps we should move under the tree?"

She nodded but didn't remove her hand from his neck.

"Sit tight, then." He tucked an arm beneath her legs, rose to his knees, then stood with her in his arms. He deposited her under the low-hanging branches. "Be right back."

Conway snatched the remains of their picnic and brought it under the tree. Then he dashed over to the horses, removed their hobbles, and led them under the willow.

"Isn't this cozy?" he asked as the horses continued grazing beneath the branches.

Helen took a deep breath as Conway dashed around collecting the blanket, basket, and horses. Her heart raced, and her lips tingled. He had said *love*. Fear and happiness raised their fists against one another within her breast. Did she love him? Or was it lust? Was she willing to take the chance?

The rain increased, and Conway returned with the

horses. He had removed his riding jacket earlier, and the linen shirt clung to his arms and chest. He peeled off the wet cravat and dropped it on the basket.

"You're shivering," he said, picking up the moderately dry jacket and covering her shoulders. "Let me warm you." His arms wrapped her tightly against his warm body.

"How can you not be cold?" she asked between shivers.

"I'm a hot-blooded Welshman, of course." He smelled faintly of spicy orange and rain. She wanted to lick his chest and see if it tasted the same. That thought sent panic racing down her spine.

She was giving in to her desire. NO! It had ended in disaster before. She couldn't, she just couldn't. Her pulse pounded in her ears, and she couldn't breathe. She needed to breathe. "I have to go." Helen pushed away from him and went to the small gray pony she'd chosen. It was new to the stable, and it was her first ride on him. "Easy, boy." She tossed the reins over his head and pulled the stirrup toward her.

"I'm sorry," she said over her shoulder. "I'm so sorry."

He hurried over, squatted down, and gave her a lift up. His hand gripped her ankle. "I pushed you too quickly. Let me apologize for frightening you. It won't happen again."

She hooked her knee around the pommel and looked down at him, tears burning her eyes. Her heart ached for both of them. "But it will, don't you see? It will happen over and over and over again." She nudged the horse with her heel, and he moved into the open, rain pelting through the thin material of her shirt.

Lightning cracked above them, and the gelding reared. Helen squeezed with her legs and held tight to the rein. The horse landed with a *thump* and took off at a gallop. Between the tears and the downpour, she couldn't see anything. Her sobs were absorbed by the hoofbeats and the gusting wind. The horse ignored her commands. She yanked on the rein with all her strength, and it did nothing to slow the beast.

Conway appeared next to her, his hand outstretched. Terror gripped her, and she shook her head.

"Take my hand," he yelled.

Helen gripped the pommel with one hand. She couldn't do it. It wasn't just an offer of help, she realized. It was the trust she would give him, and her heart would follow. *Not again. I can't go through the pain again.*

She felt his strong arm on her waist as he lifted her from the saddle. She let the rein fall away. He settled her in front of him, pulling back on his own horse until they were at a standstill. The rain had eased and was only a steady shower. The wind lessened, and the sky lightened.

"This was my dream," he muttered.

"What?"

He turned her chin, so she had to face him. His hand moved up to her cheek. "I'm not him, Helen. *I am not him.*"

Shaking her head, she pushed away from him and slid off the horse. She began running. Running from her past, running from the future. Just running until she couldn't breathe anymore. But he was there to catch her before she fell.

Conway held her up by the shoulders, his hair stuck to his face, water streaming down his back, his eyes dark and fierce. "I'm not bloody him," he yelled. "I love you. With all my heart and soul. You are all I think of, all I dream of, all I need to make my life whole. You are not an instrument to achieve my goal. *You* are my goal. *You* are my happiness."

She stood there, sucking in deep breaths of air, her dress plastered to her body, rain soaking her head. But she saw it.

Helen saw the love in his eyes. She saw the truth in his words, and she wavered.

Then he kissed her. A kiss of acceptance, of passion, of

determination. And love. He did love her, and she loved him. It was unlike any feeling she'd had in the past. The uncertainty faded, replaced with understanding. This was not the same emotion she'd had with Rory. This was her steadfast Welshman. A man who would stand by her throughout her life. A man who would love her daughter as his own.

He kissed her again, gently this time, and her body leaned into him. She soaked in his warmth, his strength. When the kiss ended, he cupped her face with his hands, and his deep brown gaze locked with hers. "Let me be the eye of your storm, Helen. Let me be your calm, secure shelter. We will always face strong winds in this life, but I'm sturdy, a rock. I will hold all three of us safe against the gales."

She saw her future in those dark, loving orbs. She saw *them,* a family. Helen nodded, her tears mixing with the rain, and threw her arms around his neck.

EPILOGUE

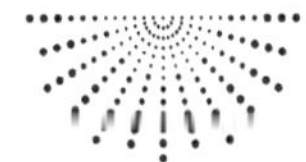

September 1821
Stanfeld Estate

Conway sat on his horse, waiting for Madoc to join him.

"Are you ready for the church, old man?" asked his half brother as he rode up.

"I've been ready longer than you know." He had tried to wipe the grin from his face earlier that morning and given up. Why not let everyone know how he felt? He was getting married to the most beautiful woman in all of England and Wales.

They had waited until the year of mourning was up, and their families could attend the ceremony. His grandmother, sister-in-law, and nephew waited in the church.

Helen was with her mother and sisters and would soon follow them.

Psst! He turned to Madoc, who was tipping his head

toward the rear of Conway's horse. He turned to see Maeve looking under the horse, and up at its belly. She was dressed in a light-rose gown, detailed with pearls and lace. A crown of greenery and flowers lay upon head, ribbons dangling down her back.

"What exactly are you doing, my little princess?" he asked, amused.

She sighed and propped her fists on her hips. "Seeing if it's a boy. If it's not, you'll have no sons, only daughters. I really want a brother." Her speech had improved greatly over the last six months.

Both men guffawed. "Well, little Maeve, since we have the proper horse, we will see you at the altar," said Madoc.

❧

Helen was surrounded by her family and those who had just become her family. Her new sister- and mother-in-law, the Dowager and Lady Breckens, were both lovely and warm. They had become friends in an instant. Conway's grandmother did not have the same tenderness in her greeting, but was cordial and welcoming.

"She's like the parmesan ice we had at Gunter's once," Helen's mother had said after they had spent a week together. "You're not sure if you like it, but the flavor grows on you."

However, Helen had seen the affection in the dowager's eyes not only when she looked at her grandson, but when she spent time with her daughter, Maeve. The little girl had charmed the older woman with her frankness, intelligence, and knowledge of Welsh folklore and superstition. Conway's grandmother wouldn't be overly affectionate, ready with hugs, but Helen knew she would be a friend and ally.

Conway's mother would provide the warmth that Helen

would miss when she left her own family. The two had instantly liked each other at their first meeting. And there was Evie, Brecken's wife, whose sister had married one of the MacNaughton clan. Gideon had reminded her that she would be just over the border, not on the Continent. Visits would be frequent.

Helen blinked at her reflection. Her dress was of the palest blue silk with an overlay of ivory Italian lace. She wore sapphires at her ears and throat, with tiny blue paste gems sparkling in her upswept hair. Tugging on her gloves, she swallowed the lump growing in her throat.

Griffith's mother sighed, blinking back tears. "You are the loveliest of brides."

"But do you have everything?" asked the soon-to-be dowager countess. "Gruff told you about the tradition?"

Helen nodded. "Something old, to ensure my friends and family will always be there when needed, is the handkerchief belonging to my grandmother. Something new, promising success in my new life, is the imported lace. Something borrowed is my mother's necklace and earbobs, so that I bring the love of my family with me. And something blue is my dress."

"It's time," her mother called. "We mustn't be late."

Her nerves were jangling, and the conversation around her was a dull roar. She heard nothing but her own fears and misgivings. She wanted to wipe her sweaty palms but didn't want to ruin her dress. And then she was entering the church, and Conway was there, smiling. And her doubts evaporated. He was the man she had always wanted. The man who would make her and Maeve his world. She'd never felt more certain than when joining hands with the Earl of Griffith. She barely remembered any of the words during the ceremony except "I will." And she would love this man with all her heart until her last breath.

The wedding fulfilled all her childhood dreams. As they left the church, the guests calling and cheering, Helen heard the church bells toll. She looked up, for they hadn't paid for the bell ringer. To her surprise, Conway bent and whispered in her ear, "An old Welsh superstition. Church bells that are rung for a wedding will keep the storms away." Then he kissed her cheek and gave her a wink.

Oh, how she loved this kind, sweet, obstinate man. There would be more storms, of course. But they would weather each one together. *Yes, Papa,* Helen thought as she looked up at her beaming husband. The love was so evident in his eyes that she thought her heart would burst.

The sun *will* always shine again with this man by her side.

Reviews are the lifeblood of authors. If you've enjoyed this story, please consider leaving a few words at your favorite retailer.

Keep updated on future releases, exclusive excerpts, and prizes by following my newsletter:

https://www.subscribepage.com/k3f1z5

Once Upon a Widow series

Earl of Sunderland

A Wicked Earl's Widow

Rhapsody and Rebellion (Gideon, Lord Stanfeld, and Lissie Craigg)

Earl of Darby

Earl of Brecken (Madoc and Evie Franklin)

. . .

Fenella's story and the story of Lord Raines are in my A MacNaughton Castle Romance This is a steamy series.

A Merry MacNaughton Mishap (holiday prequel, Calum MacNaughton and Peigi Craigg)

Deception and Desire #1 (Lachlan MacNaughton and Fenella Franklin)

An Allusive Love #2 (Brodie MacNaughton and Kirsty MacDunn)

A Bonny Pretender #3 (Frank, Viscount Raines, and Brigid MacNaughton)

ABOUT AUBREY WYNNE

USA Today Bestselling author Aubrey Wynne resides in the Midwest with her husband, dogs, horses, mule, and barn cats. Obsessions include wine, history, travel, trail riding, and all things Christmas. Her Chicago Christmas series has received multiple awards and was twice nominated as a Rone finalist by InD'tale Magazine.

Aubrey's first love is medieval romance but after dipping her toe in the Regency period in 2018 with the *Wicked Earls' Club,* she was smitten. This inspired her spin-off series *Once Upon a Widow*. In 2020, she launched the Scottish Regency series *A MacNaughton Castle Romance* with Dragonblade Novels.

Social Media Links:

Website:
http://www.aubreywynne.com
Facebook:
https://www.facebook.com/magnificentvalor
Aubrey's Ever After Facebook group:

https://www.facebook.com/groups/AubreyWynnesEverAfters/

Twitter:

https://twitter.com/Aubreywynne51

Pinterest:

https://www.pinterest.com/aubreywynne51/

Instagram:

https://www.instagram.com/Aubreywynne51

Bookbub page:

https://www.bookbub.com/profile/aubrey-wynne

Goodreads:

https://www.goodreads.com/author/show/7383937.Aubrey_Wynne

Sign up for my newsletter and don't miss future releases

https://www.subscribepage.com/k3f1z5

SNEAK PEEK AT RHAPSODY AND REBELLION

"Those who dream by day are cognizant of many things which escape those who dream only by night."

— EDGAR ALLEN POE

Chapter One

August 16, 1819

Stanfeld Estate,

County of Norfolk, England

Gideon touched the horse's flank with his boot, moving into a smooth, rocking canter as he focused on the distant stone wall. His muscular body moved with the gelding, his thighs gripping the saddle, and his hands resting lightly on the reins. Still in training, Verity had been worth every pound. He had heart and courage and would gallop over a cliff if asked.

Marked as a rogue and a bone-setter at Tattersall's auction, the horse had apparently refused to bend under training or listen to the whip. But the gelding's eyes had held intelligence when Gideon stroked his wavy dark forelock and blew gently on his nose. The "beast" turned out to have more common sense than most of those roughriders, who thought to break an animal's spirit with fear and domination. The three-year-old wanted to please but had rebelled against unwarranted pain. The fading scars that marked the ebony hide from sharp spurs and countless lashes proved it had not been the proper incentive. Verity enjoyed a challenge and learned quickly when asked with kindness. Animals weren't much different from people really, except perhaps more trustworthy.

The pair approached the hedgerow. Gideon leaned forward and

grabbed a fistful of mane with his spur hand. A subtle cue and the horse sailed over the shrub, landing gracefully on the other side. The wind pulled at the opening in his shirt, and it billowed around him with a flapping noise. He gave Verity a pat on the neck and eased him into a trot. "Good boy!"

The cool morning breeze lifted the hair off Gideon's neck and cooled the sweat running down his back. The sweet smell of fresh-cut hay filled the air and he breathed deeply. His eyes swept over the green pastures and dotted hills that had claimed his imagination as a child. Playing with the village children and fighting dragons on ancient ponies, looking for buried treasure, or going to war against the Danes or the French—depending on the most recent history lesson. Where had that adventurous youth gone?

Verity's ears pricked forward. Gideon chuckled at the scruffy little brown mutt bounding up the hill. "Good morn to you, Little Bit."

The dog barked in reply, his tail wagging so rapidly that it seemed a blur. "A race, you say?" Little Bit barked his agreement. "I'll tell you what. I'll keep him in a trot to make it fair."

The threesome ambled west, their backs to the sun. They crested a hill and the sight of his childhood home in the distance, standing sentry over the countryside, filled Gideon with pride. The numerous windows of the imposing three-story medieval manor glinted and flashed like jewels in a crown of gray sandstone. On each corner, gable, and the entrance sat miniature turrets like arrows pointing to the heavens. Surrounded by the original moat, it reminded visitors of long-gone knights, fair maidens, and chivalry. A wide, arched bridge spanned the ditch, bricks matching the color of the mansion and providing ample entrance to the estate grounds. Rolling hills and grazing pastures surrounded the mansion on three sides with acres of forest along the back. From atop this hill, it was an impressive sight, and Gideon always enjoyed watching people's reaction the first time they saw it.

Little Bit barked, tail wagging and feet pawing at his stirrup. "My father passed on quite a legacy, didn't he? Now it's up to me to maintain and improve it."

He leaned down to give the dog a final scratch then headed down the hill at an easy canter, mentally ticking off the correspondence he would respond to after breakfast. The estate's steward also wanted to update him on some newly acquired livestock. There was the appointment with the solicitor next week in London concerning the textile mill in Glasgow. The business had been his father's personal project so Gideon was eager to learn more about the details of that particular investment. It was the only corner of the Stanfeld holdings the late earl had seen to himself.

London. The visit would be a two-edged sword. On one hand, he looked forward to a few nights of gaming and camaraderie with good friends. Perhaps a stop at Tattersall's to see what was on the auction block. On the other hand, those voracious, title-seeking mothers with their simpering single daughters… At least the families were sparser this time of year. At twenty-five, he still enjoyed his bachelor status and tried to avoid the town in the spring and early summer as carefully as horse piles on a busy street.

Just before crossing the bridge, he dismounted. Little Bit rushed ahead, barking a warning that his master was home. Gideon paused beneath one of the yew trees flanking the bridge, tucked his shirt into his breeches, and rolled down his sleeves. The reddish brown bark shown with purple in the morning light, and the low hanging branches swayed softly in the breeze. He walked across the bridge, buttoning his cuffs, his boot heels clicking against the bricks. The water below sparkled as lilies floated lazily along, an occasional fish making a splash. A stable hand waited on the steps, holding a crust of bread out to the dog.

"Give him a long rubdown. He worked hard this morning." Gideon gave the horse another pat on its muscular neck and handed over the reins.

"Yes, my lord." The man led the animal away, the tatty pup at his heels.

Sanders, the butler, greeted him at the door. "Good day, my lord. Lady Stanfeld is waiting for you." His gray eyes, matching his thinning hair, danced with humor as he collected his lord's waistcoat, crop, and gloves. "She appears to be making a list."

Gideon groaned. "Of females?"

"Yes, my lord, I'm afraid so."

"Thank you, Sanders." Gideon ignored the family portraits and the suit of armor stoically standing guard as he strode through the entryway. Intent on changing before greeting his mother, he bounded up the circular staircase two steps at a time.

Gideon entered his chambers, finished a quick half-bath, and wiped dry with a clean linen towel. He dressed in fresh buckskin breeches, a white cambric shirt, a brandy-colored waistcoat, and finished tying his cravat as he hurried down the stairs.

"Good morning, dear Mama," he murmured as he bent low to kiss her cheek. "You look fetching in that deep shade of lavender. I'm happy to see you finally out of those blacks. It doesn't suit you."

"I've followed the English tradition of mourning in honor of your father. But I'm happy to have some color back. It brightens the skin." Her words still held the barest hint of a Scottish accent. Maeve smoothed her crepe skirt and smiled. "I've been waiting for you."

"So I've been told. Perhaps some coffee before you bombard me with your list?" Gideon smirked at her surprised look until those dark blue eyes flashed with determination. He held up a hand. "I'll listen with interest as soon as I've finished a cup and had something to eat."

Maeve watched in bemused silence as a servant poured the steaming black liquid into a china cup. Gideon lathered soft butter onto a thick slice of fresh bread and scooped some cherry preserves on top. With a groan of delight, he chewed with his eyes closed and finished with a smack of his lips. "This season's cherries were superb."

Maeve opened her mouth then closed it as he reached for his coffee. She made a face.

"And is that displeasure aimed at me, Mama?"

She shook her head. "I don't know how you can prefer that horrible drink to tea. And without even a drop of milk or lump of sugar."

He grinned, spearing a piece of cold beef with his fork. "I have my father's dour demeanor and prefer the bitter to the sweet. Now, who is on your marriage agenda?"

She frowned. "It is not an agenda or about marriage. I've decided to have a small dinner party, and I've listed a few names that might be of interest."

The last thing Gideon wanted was to be surrounded by tiresome young ladies looking for a husband. But seeing the light back in his mother's eyes, he kept his thoughts to himself. It had been over a year since she had accepted an invitation or entertained. He was willing to be the sacrificial lamb to see her reenter society.

"I am happy to play host for whatever event you would like to arrange. Now about that list..."

His mind wandered as she told him of the families that would receive an invitation. His father had endured these social affairs as a matter of course. Always the proper gentleman, always the mannered aristocrat, always the impassive Englishman. Life was a set of rules and one followed those tenets to the letter in private, in social circles, and in business. The world, according to the late earl, was black and white.

The exception had been his wife, the vibrant and outspoken Maeve of the prominent Clan MacNaughton. The earl had disliked the superstitious and rebellious Highlanders but had fallen in love with one of the chieftain's daughters. She had seemed to be the only weakness in his inflexible world, the only person or thing he allowed to let him stray from society's rigid rules. Gideon had seen her pull caps with him and hold her own, occasionally even winning an argument. Those instances had ended with a wicked glint in his father's eyes and a smug smile on his mother's lips. Then the two of them would hide away in their bedchamber the rest of the day.

"I received a letter from Marietta last week. She'd like to visit before winter. So I will plan it as a welcome dinner in September. She's finally with child, you know. It may be quite some time before she can travel again."

The last words sounded wistful and brought Gideon back to the conversation. Marietta, the eldest sister, was less than two years behind him. Then came Charlotte, four years his junior, and Helen the youngest at nineteen. All had married well, in their father's opinion, with the exception of Helen. She had wed a wealthy baseborn Irishman. "It will be good to see Etta again. I'm surprised Lord Burnham is allowing her out of his sight. After three years, I swear the man is still smelling of April and May."

"There is nothing wrong with being in love. And he'll most certainly keep a close eye on that girl." Maeve laughed. "She's still a bit impetuous, but motherhood will slow her down."

"I hope something does." He rose from the table and kissed Maeve again on the cheek. "I will leave you to your preparations, then. I'll be with the steward for the rest of the day. "

***

The accounts for the quarter completed, Gideon and Jethro Birks admired the sheep littering the grassy hillside. They were fine stock and his steward had finagled an excellent price the previous year. "Outstanding job. I'm impressed with the results of the spring shearing. Damn good wool and damn good profits."

"It took some talking, my lord, but I finally convinced your father to let me bring in these sheep from Gower. Much better quality than the Vale long wool and brings twice the price." The summer sun had bleached Jethro's hair almost white, making his brown eyes and tanned skin appear even darker. He pointed in the direction of a southern pasture. "I'd like to try grazing the cattle same as the sheep. Get the animals out of the yards, and we'll see better milk and beef."

"With your past record, I'm inclined to trust your judgment on this. By god, you even managed a second hay cutting this summer. There'll be plenty of feed for the winter."

"Can't take all the credit for that, my lord. The weather helped a bit."

Gideon looked over the acreage with a contented smile, his father's words coming to mind. *Surround yourself with competent men, treat them well, and your land and finances will prosper.*

This was proof of that philosophy. He'd known Jethro since they were boys, hunting squirrel with slingshots and swimming in the horse pond. He was the third generation of Birks to manage the Stanfeld estates, and Gideon was thankful to have such a downy steward.

"I'll be in London for a few days, checking in with the solicitor. Fair warning"—he cleared his throat—"Lady Stanfeld has come out of mourning and is planning a country party for September. What she has described as a small dinner gathering will no doubt turn into a week of company."

"Yes, my lord. Consider me prepared for the upcoming requests."

"Give my regards to your charming wife." Gideon turned his gelding back toward the manor. It had been a productive day, and he was ready for a glass of sherry and a good meal.

***

The Countess of Stanfeld settled into her favorite chair near the library hearth. She held a small book of poems and read a few pages until her eyes grew weary. Her thoughts strayed to her late husband Charles and the heart condition that had sapped his strength his last years. It had made him weak of body but not weak of mind. He had remained lucid and pragmatic until the end, knowing death was upon him and looking the reaper in the eye. Maeve had always admired his supreme will and saw that same strength in her children.

But he had also been a narrow-minded man in a sense, whose rational views did not allow him to see anything except what lay in front of him. If it was not factual or quantifiable, it was not real. He had laughed at her first vision of a sinking ship he planned to invest in, indulging her recount as if it were an amusing story. Until it came true. It had shaken the very foundation of everything he considered Truth. Rather than look too deeply into the situation, he shunned the unexplainable. Ran from it as if it were the devil himself after his soul.

His reaction had been swift and irrevocable. Her female mind was too easily swayed by homeland folklore. Maeve would not return to the Highlands while there was breath left in him. She would remain in England, become a proper countess, and forget the mystical nonsense of her childhood. By that time, she loved him so deeply that the fear in his eyes had frightened her also. He didn't understand, didn't have the capability to conceive of something so intangible, other than God. And he struggled with that omniscient presence. So she never told him of another vision, and instead did what she could to avoid tragedy whenever possible. She willingly gave up her childhood home for him but refused to give up her family.

The earl had compromised with his wife and in-laws by going to the Scottish Lowlands and meeting in Glasgow twice a year. The couple had first been introduced in that city, when Charles and her father, Calum MacNaughton, had met to discuss the purchase of a textile mill. Her father still insisted the papers had only been signed after Maeve had agreed to his courtship. The trips satisfied the desire for her children to know the MacNaughton clan. Gideon had always been especially close to his grandfather, growing more like his image every year with Calum's muscular build, black hair, and piercing blue eyes.

She smiled, closed her eyes, and gave in to a pleasant afternoon nap.

He pushed against the throng of men, women, and children to hear the gentleman on the stage. The stink of unwashed bodies and a hum of excitement filled the air. He pulled off his waistcoat as the sweat pooled beneath his collar. The speaker's words of reform and the right to vote echoed in his head and filled him with purpose.

A woman holding a small child sidled up next to him, a smile on her lips. The pair made him think of his own wife and the family they would have. The wee girl had the same dimples as her mother. The babe waved a hand at him, and he caught her chubby fingers in his. Grasping her mother's braid in her other hand, the babe sucked heartily then began to cry as the noise increased. She squealed as the crowd jostled the pair and reached toward him. The pressure of bodies behind them intensified, and the hair on the back of his neck rose. Something wasna right.

Screams pierced the air, and he turned to see the cause of such panic. Mounted Hussars stormed the assembly, the rhythmic whisk of blades slicing the air. A glistening black beast, eyes rolling, lunged forward then reared. Flying hooves pawed at the scrambling bodies and struck the infant in the head. The mother screamed, her arms reaching for the falling child.

He pushed the frantic woman away from the soldier's sword then threw himself on the tiny, lifeless form. "Ye bloody bastards," he cried as the horse reared once again.

This time its full weight landed on his back. The crack of bone echoed in his ears. Excruciating pain exploded along the length of his body. From the ground, he saw a jumble of feet and hooves, all moving in different directions. A man's face—contorted in pain—trampled by the frantic feet escaping the massacre. He tried to hunch over the child still beneath him, protect it from the stampede, but his body had been flattened. An image flashed of the local butcher pounding a tough piece of meat.

A blow to his head...a piercing throb... Then the world spun in slow motion. The shrieks of victims and harsh shouts of the soldiers came from far away now. Another image. His sweet wife's face.

"I'm so verra sorry, Lissie..." he whispered.

***

Gideon entered the library, still warm from the afternoon sun. Mama sat before the fireplace, the large wingback almost swallowing up her small frame. She had aged in the last year. A few streaks of gray now blended with the rich auburn hair. Her eyes were closed, but her lids fluttered as if dreaming. The sapphire ring, a wedding gift from her husband that matched her eyes, glinted and winked as her slender fingers gripped and released the armchair. Her head rocked back and forth as Gideon squatted down next to her. His fingers covered hers, and he squeezed to wake her from such troubled sleep. The touch sent a jolt through her body. Her eyes snapped open.

"No!" she gasped, her gaze fixed on the darkened hearth.

"Mama, you were dreaming." His thumb stroked the top of her hand, his voice soft and soothing. "Look at me, Mama, and you will see."

Maeve slowly turned her head, tears now spilling down her cheeks. "Oh Gideon, it was ghastly."

"What did you dream?"

"It was not a dream." Her voice faltered. "Your cousin, Ian, is dead."

"What? Did you receive a letter from Scotland?" Gideon had not seen any correspondence from his mother's family over the last week, and nothing had arrived today.

"I do not need a letter. I saw it. There's been a terrible slaughter in Manchester, and Ian was trampled..." She lifted her chin and wiped at her wet cheeks with determination. "You must take me home to my clan."

"To the Highlands? You haven't been there since your wedding." He sighed and rubbed the back of his neck. "I can't just run off to Scotland with my aging mother because of a dream."

"Aging?" Her eyes narrowed, anger shining from beneath her lashes. "I have more stamina than most of those mutton-headed females of the *ton*."

He had to agree with her but bit back a smile. "This is folly. A trick of the mind from lack of sleep." He pressed his lips to her fingers. "Let's have a glass of sherry, and you'll feel better after we eat."

"Don't patronize me. Your father didn't believe in…" She took his face in both her hands, strength growing in her touch and her gaze steady and direct. "It doesn't matter. Listen to me. It was not a dream but a message of sorts that we are needed at home."

"This is our home." Gideon stood and leaned an arm against the fireplace mantel, worried the past year had also taken a toll on her mind. An uprising in Manchester? There had been rumblings throughout parts of the country but nothing significant.

"This is *your* home. *Mine* has always been in Scotland, regardless of how long I've been away." Her eyes pleaded with him.

"What about Marietta's visit in September?" That would end this foolishness, he was sure.

"It will have to wait until October. You must promise we will leave as soon as you return from London. Or I will go alone."

He looked up to the ceiling, hoping for some divine intervention. None came. "I give you my word."

ALSO BY AUBREY WYNNE

Once Upon a Widow (Sweet Regency Series)

Earl of Sunderland #1

Maggie award, International Digital Awards finalist

Christopher Roker inherited the title of rake. She hides behind her independence. Fate accepts the challenge...

Escaping his late brother's memory, Lady Grace is a welcome distraction. But as the attraction grows, Kit finds himself wavering between his old military life and the lure of an exceptional but unwilling woman.

A Wicked Earl's Widow #2

Recommended by InD'tale Magazine

Eliza, Lady Sunderland, is widowed after one year. Her abusive father, near financial ruin, is already planning another wedding.

When Viscount Pendleton discovers a beauty defending an elderly woman against ruffians, he is smitten. But Nate soon realizes he must discover Eliza's dark past to save the woman he loves.

Rhapsody and Rebellion Book #3

Maggie finalist, nominated for Rone Award, InD'tale Magazine

A Scottish legacy... A political rebellion... Two hearts destined to meet...

Alisabeth was betrothed from the cradle. At seventeen, she marries her best friend and finds happiness if not passion. In less than a year, a political rebellion makes her a widow. The handsome English earl arrives a month later and rouses her desire and a terrible guilt.

Crossing the border into Scotland, Gideon finds his predictable world turned upside down. Folklore, legend, and political unrest intertwine with an unexpected attraction to a feisty Highland beauty. When the earl learns of an English plot to stir the Scots into rebellion, he must choose his country or save the clan and the woman who stirs his soul.

Earl of Darby #4

Holt Medallion Winner, NTRWA Reader's Choice Award, Nominated for Rone Award, InD'tale magazine

Miss Hannah Pendleton, nursing her pride after her childhood crush falls in love with another, hurls herself into the excitement of a first season.

Since his wife's suicide on their wedding night, the Earl of Darby has carefully cultivated his rakish reputation. But when Nicholas sees a lovely newcomer being courted by the devil himself, her innocence and candor revive the chivalry buried deep in his soul.

Earl of Brecken #5

He's on the brink of ruin. She's in search of a hero.

Notorious for his seductive charm, the Earl of Brecken searches for a wealthy heiress. His choices are dismal until he meets Miss Franklin. Guileless, gorgeous and with an enormous dowry, she seems the answer to his prayers. Until his conscience makes an unexpected appearance.

Earl of Griffith #6

Sorrow and Regrets...

After eloping, a widowed Lady Helen is disillusioned with love and raising a three-year-old alone. Now she must face the music and her family.

An unexpected ray of sunshine...

Conway, Earl of Griffith is smitten at first sight with his friend's sister and adorable daughter. But can he convince the grieving and lovely widow that love is worth a second chance?

Beware A Wallflower's Wrath #7

Annis Craigg gave her heart—and innocence—away at seventeen. When Lord Robert Harding returns to Scotland fifteen years later, he's desperate to find the only woman he's ever loved. But she has secrets and an attitude.

Lies, secrets, and betrayal will challenge the fierce love of a steadfast Highlander and remorseful but determined Englishman. Will destiny find a way to bring two star-crossed souls together?

A MacNaughton Castle Romance series

"Witty and sensual!"

"Lovely characters and complicated family conflicts. You will easily get caught up in their lives."

— GOODREADS REVIEW

A Merry MacNaughton Mishap (Prequel)

Rone finalist, InD'tale Magazine, N.N. Light Book Heaven finalist

When Calum MacNaughton rescues a rival clan member from an icy drowning, he is unexpectedly rewarded with the clansman's most precious possession. Now Calum has until Twelfth Night to convince her to stay.

Deception and Desire #1

Nominated for Rone award, InD'tale Magazine, N.N. Light Book Heaven award winner

Two rebellious souls... An innocent deception... One scorching catastrophe...

Fenella Franklin's talents lie in numbers and a keen business mind, not in the art of flirtation. Lachlan MacNaughton has neither the temperament nor the patience to be the next MacNaughton chief, preferring to knock heads together rather than placate bickering clansmen. Their attraction sparks a passion they cannot deny. But will an innocent deception test their newfound love?

Allusive Love #2

A woman in love... An infuriating Scot... A tantalizing chase.

Kirstine has loved Brodie MacNaughton forever, but he considers Kirsty his best friend. When he turns to her for advice, she surprises him with an unexpected kiss that sends fire through his veins. When pride, Highland politics, and tragedy collide, he realizes how precious and allusive true love can be.

A Bonny Pretender #3

She's pretending to be someone she's not... His entire life is based on a lie...

Brigid MacNaughton becomes the perfect lady to placate her family, then falls in love with a quiet, self-possessed Englishman. Lord Raines is smitten with the beguiling and demure Scot. If he divulges his scandalous parentage, will she still fall willingly into his arms? Bonny pretender vs handsome imposter... Can love overcome a double deception?

A Medieval Encounter Series

Rolf's Quest

Great Expectations winner, Fire & Ice, Maggie finalist

"Romance, destiny, family values & betrayal all played parts in this intriguing novel that had me turning each page in anticipation."

— *THE BOOKTWEETER*

A wizard, a curse, a fated love...

When Rolf finally discovers the woman who can end the curse that has plagued his family for centuries, she is already betrothed. Time is running out for the royal wizard of King Henry II. If he cannot find true love without the use of sorcery, the magic will die for future generations.

Melissa is intrigued by the mystical, handsome man who haunts her by night and tempts her by day. His bizarre tale of Merlin, enchantments, and finding genuine love has her questioning his sanity and her heart.

From the moment Melissa stepped from his dreams and into his arms, Rolf knew she was his destiny. Now, he will battle against time, a powerful duke, and call on the gods to save her.

Saving Grace (Contemporary/Colonial America)

Holt and Maggie finalist

This unique piece has the reader traveling between the early 1700s and the early 2000s with ease and amazement. The audience truly feels sorrow for Grace and Chloe and is able to connect with each woman for the hardships they are overcoming… The attention to historical facts and details leave one breathless, especially upon learning the people from the past did exist and the memorial erected still stands.

— *IND'TALE MAGAZINE*

A tortured soul meets a shattered heart...

Chloe Hicks' life consisted of an egocentric ex-husband, a pile of bills, and an equine business in foreclosure until a fire destroys the stable and her beloved ranch horse. After the marshal suspects arson, she escapes the accusing eyes of her hometown.

Jackson Hahn, the local historian, distracts Chloe with a 17th-century legend of a woman wrongly accused of witchcraft. It might explain the ghostly happenings on the property. She is drawn to the similarities that plagued both their lives. Perhaps the past can help heal the present. But danger lurks in the shadows...

Made in United States
Troutdale, OR
06/11/2024

20491000R00098